BOOKS BY RICKY FRY

He Comes in the Night
Lionshead
Bill and Ty Get High

HE COMES IN THE NIGHT

RICKY FRY

For Lucian, who held my hand
while I slept on the bus.

There was once a time when vampires were as common as leaves of grass, or berries in a pail, and they never kept still, but wandered round at night among the people.

— A Story from Botoşani

HE COMES
IN THE NIGHT

ONE

Nancy Hardaway was in bed, propped against a pillow with the latest Vanity Fair clutched in her pencil-thin fingers, when she was startled by a loud thump coming from Baby Nora's nursery. She lowered the magazine to her lap and nudged her sleeping husband.

"Byron," she said, "something isn't right in the nursery. Go and see what's happened."

Mr. Hardaway groaned and rolled over beneath the heavy comforter. "It's probably just the nanny, my love. Maybe she dropped something."

Whatever the nanny dropped must have been very heavy to make such a terrible noise. Just once, she thought, it would be nice to have a proper night's sleep. Baby Nora had been nothing but trouble since they brought her home from Massachusetts General Hospital. It had only been six months, but Nancy Hardaway was thoroughly exhausted.

The nanny was supposed to make life easier. Compared to most first-time mothers, Nancy had taken a decidedly hands-off role in the raising of their daughter. She'd stopped breast-feeding the moment Nora's first teeth had appeared, pumping milk with an expensive device and switching to formula not long after. It was an easy decision. She couldn't stand the way Nora chewed and bit her nipples.

Tonight she was especially tired, and had hoped to get some rest before the charity fundraiser she'd be attending with Mr. Hardaway the following evening. The high society ladies could be so judgmental, and she didn't dare show her face without at least eight hours of beauty sleep. The years had been kind to her, but still, she wasn't getting any younger. After nearly a decade of trying with no luck, Baby Nora was a surprise. The last thing Nancy Hardaway had expected was to become a mother on the eve of her thirty-seventh birthday.

She listened again for any sign of the nanny stirring in the nursery, but there was only silence. She thought there should at least be footsteps, the sound of the young but plump nanny passing through the corridor on the way back to her room. And Nora—there had never been a baby who cried as often as Nora. Such a disturbance would certainly have woken her.

Thank goodness the sleeping pill she'd taken before settling in with her magazine had yet to work its modern magic. Just a quick check of the nursery and she'd be drifting off to sleep in a matter of minutes. She had an especially big day tomorrow. Though there were few things she loved more than socializing at charity events, they were always so much trouble.

She felt her way along the corridor in the dark, until she found the switch. The long hall was empty, the nursery to one side and the nanny's room opposite. The nanny's door was open. Nancy leaned over the threshold and peered inside. The light beside the bed was still on but there was no sign of the young woman. Perhaps, she thought, she was still in the nursery tending to Nora.

She stopped to listen outside the nursery door. It was strange, the old house being so quiet. The door creaked as she pushed it open and a chill ran down her spine. In the faint glow of an old table lamp, she saw a plump figure spread on the floor beside the crib. The twisted face of the nanny stared up at her, a look of horror frozen in her motionless eyes.

Nancy Hardaway screamed. She'd never seen a dead body in real life before, but the young nanny certainly looked very dead. A slight trickle of blood oozed from the lifeless woman's mouth and pooled on the hardwood floor beneath her.

"What is it, Nancy?" Mr. Hardaway appeared in the doorway with a golf club in his hand.

"She's dead, Byron. She's dead." It was the only thing she could think to say.

"Call 9-1-1." He knelt beside the bleeding woman and shook her limp body, called her by a first name his wife had never once used during the nanny's short time in their employ.

Nancy couldn't move. She couldn't think. As she watched her husband pumping up and down on the young woman's chest, the only thing that filled the panicked space of her mind was the loud thump that had surely been the woman's body as she keeled over on the hardwood floor.

And there, in the crib at the center of the room, Baby Nora smiled up at her—a tiny bundle wrapped in swaddling blankets—with a peculiar look of satisfaction on her glowing, angelic face.

It was only later, long after the flashing lights and siren of the ambulance had pulled away from the Federalist façade of their Beacon Hill townhouse, that the Hardaways learned their daughter's nanny was indeed quite dead. They'd have to wait for the official report, of course, but the investigator from the medical examiner's office said it appeared as though she'd died of a sudden brain hemorrhage. "It's quite rare," he told them, "for someone of such a young age."

"Oh, dear." Nancy thought it was terrible. She wondered what the other society women would say. As far as she could recall, no one had ever lost a nanny before, with the exception of the McDowell's nanny, who'd died in her sleep. But the tough old Scottish woman had been seventy-nine, long overdue for retirement. Such things happen, and nobody had faulted Lisa McDowell.

"We've been unable to locate her family," said the investigator. "Perhaps you have their contact information, or at least something we might find useful?"

She was almost ashamed to admit she knew so little of the woman who'd spent the previous three months sleeping under their roof. "I'm sorry. I was never very good about those things."

"I see." He scratched his chin and scribbled notes in a little pad. "Did she ever mention anything to you about her state of health?"

"What do you mean?" Nancy had always just assumed the young woman was perfectly normal, if not slightly overweight.

"Was she unwell? Did she say anything or visit a doctor?" He'd already searched the nanny's room for any signs of a health condition and had found nothing, not even a bottle of aspirin.

Nancy still wasn't thinking clearly after such a distressing incident, but she recalled a conversation they'd had in the kitchen one morning while Inez, the Hardaway's long-time housekeeper, prepared breakfast. It was difficult to forget the look of fear that had gripped the young woman's face.

"She'd complained of having frequent nightmares—such terrible nightmares."

The investigator didn't look up as he continued writing in his notepad. "What sort of nightmares?"

"She wouldn't mention specifics." It was true. The nanny had been reluctant to describe the nature of her terrifying nighttime visions. "She'd wake in a fright. I heard her screaming from our bedroom down the hall."

"Interesting." He scratched his chin again. "I'm not sure it has anything to do with a brain hemorrhage, but we appreciate any details you can provide."

"Of course." She'd considered firing the nanny on more than one occasion—on the nights when she'd been woken by the woman's screams. Nora's frequent crying was bad enough. Her husband had convinced her otherwise, if only to save themselves the trouble of finding a new nanny. But a new nanny was now exactly what they needed.

The investigator finished taking notes and they were left alone in the quiet space of the house. Nora was sound asleep. Nancy, whose sleeping pill had finally taken effect, was utterly exhausted from their ordeal.

It was nearly morning. The high society ladies of Boston would surely notice her absence at the charity event, but it would be even worse to explain the sudden death of their nanny. She imagined their faces—wrinkles smoothed over by Botox injections—as they feigned sympathy, each secretly delighted it hadn't happened to them.

"Oh, Byron." She rested a hand on her husband's broad shoulder. "This has all been so dreadful. What am I going to tell the ladies?"

"It could be worse."

"How could things possibly be worse than this?"

"Just think," he said. "At least you're not the nanny."

TWO

The forest had always been there, stretching out in all directions and encircling the village like the mountains that encircled the forest. The trees were old, older than the most distant memories of the village elders. Each held a forgotten secret, stories of pain and suffering, blood and tears.

The tiny village, with its collection of cobbled stone houses, was the only home Bogdan had ever known. He sat alone on a fallen tree at the edge of the forest clearing and watched the others—men and women in their finest clothes, preparing for the annual sacrifice that ensured their safety from the darkness beyond. Young girls busied themselves with baskets, heavy and overflowing with food, while the older boys, many the same age as him, built a large pyre of dry logs in the center of the village. Everyone had a role to play in what would come. Soon it would be his turn.

That night he ate like a prince. The finest foods, fresh fruit from the orchards and the roasted meat of a young goat, were served to him by the most beautiful girls of the village. The men told stories of his bravery. The women sang songs in his honor. He would be remembered as a hero, they said, for a thousand years.

Maybe it was true. But as the night grew long, he felt less like a hero and more like a martyr. It was his family's turn to make the ritual sacrifice, and as the oldest among his brothers and sisters, his fate had been sealed at the very moment of his birth. He'd long ago come to accept it, never bothering with plans or dreams of the future. Often, when he'd gone for one of his long, rambling walks deep in the forest, he'd even considered it a blessing. For him there would be no uncertainty, no growing old, no illness to eat away at him slowly until there was nothing left but a dusty bag of bones. Nobody sang songs about old men.

Still, he couldn't help feeling afraid. He wondered if it would be painful. He wondered if it was true, what the priest had said, that God would take his soul to live forever in heaven. He wondered if he would ever see his family again.

He filled his cup with dark, sweet wine and drank. It was little comfort. The hour of his death was almost upon him. But first, the wedding, in which he would be joined in eternal union with the oldest daughter of another family.

It was their way, a custom as old as the sacrifice—a holy union that strengthened the bonds within their fragile community.

The crowd cheered as she was presented, beautiful and trembling and resplendent in her white gown, the edges embroidered with bright red designs of flowers and eagles and dragons. A crown of knotted wildflowers adorned her long blonde hair—white and pure as fresh snow. Like him, she too would make a sacrifice, destined to spend the rest of her life as a widow in mourning, unable to remarry.

When it was time, the village priest led them both to the altar—it had been carried outside the little wooden church for the occasion—and bound their hands with a thin strip of white cloth. He read from the Bible until, one after the other, they repeated the sacred vows of marriage. Again the crowd cheered, as husband and wife were led together to the house and the fur-lined bed that had been prepared for the final consecration of their sacred marriage. And then they were alone.

The vows had come easily. He'd always loved her, ever since that distant summer day when he'd tied a dandelion stem into a ring and placed it upon her finger. They were only children then, playing together in a muddy field. She'd slipped and fallen in the wet mud, and when he bent down to offer help she leaned forward and kissed him.

"Bogdan?" She stroked his cheek with the back of her hand, a delicate touch that slowed his racing heart. "Are you afraid?"

He stared back at her with matching blue eyes. It hurt, the sight of her beauty. She would be the last, and the most beautiful thing he'd ever see. "Yes," he said. "I'm afraid of losing you."

"You can never lose me," she said. "I'm yours forever."

They lowered themselves together to the bed and embraced. It was the first time, in all those years spent together attending to the needs of daily life in the village, that they'd touched each other that way.

He slid the embroidered gown gently from her shoulders and looked to her once more for approval.

She nodded silently.

They moved together in the dark, their bodies joining as one to form two halves made whole. There was no past and no tomorrow, no hopeless thoughts of what would come. There was only the infinite space of the present moment, perfect and complete.

He left something of himself inside of her—a seed which might one day carry his name into the future. When it was over, they remained together, locked in tight embrace, each listening to the gentle sound of the other's breath. Then a knock came upon the door, and they knew it was time for him to go.

"Remember," she said, "I'm with you, my love."

"And I with you."

The men of the village led him to edge of the forest, near the place where he'd sat earlier in the day, while the women consoled her. He was tied to a tree just beyond the clearing, his arms secured at his sides with thick leather cords that left him unable to move.

The priest anointed his forehead with holy water and made the sign of the cross. "I deliver your soul, dear Bogdan, son of Bogdan, into the waiting arms of the Holy Spirit."

The man in the black robe turned to address the villagers who had gathered to witness the ceremony. "Three hundred years ago, in a great castle in the mountains to the south, lived a prince whose story would be told throughout the centuries. His heart was as black as the blackest night. His soul was damned. His unspeakable acts of cruelty were known throughout the land. This most unholy of princes desired, like all evil men desire, to defy our Lord God and live forever."

A murmur erupted from the crowd, expressions of deep disapproval.

The priest raised his hands in order to silence them. "To achieve his ends, the prince ordered the first-born son of each family brought to the castle, where they were slaughtered one-by-one. He ate their meat and drank their blood. He bathed in it night after night. But still he grew older. And so he summoned their youngest sons to the castle, with the hope of stealing their youth and virility.

"But the people, still mourning their terrible loss, refused to send their youngest sons to die for the evil prince. They sent word among themselves and raised a militia. When the prince learned of their resistance, he ordered his soldiers into the fields to burn their villages. Many good lives were lost. But the villagers, depleted as they were, prevailed, and stormed the castle with pitchforks and torches.

"They found him hiding beneath his bed, and hanged him by a long rope from the parapets. His head was severed and burned, his body buried in a lead-lined casket deep within the earth. But the prince's soul, so evil as it was, could pass neither to Heaven nor to Hell. It roamed the lands untethered to its mortal body, attacking them as they slept. And so the prince, who had sought eternal life among the living, found it in death."

A heavy silence had fallen over everything. The only sound Bogdan heard was his own blood, beating in his ears like a deafening thunder. Almost, he thought, the moment had almost come.

"For a hundred years," said the priest, "he terrorized the land that had once been his princely estate. Men who were healthy fell suddenly ill and died. Woman and children succumbed to his evil spirit. Villages perished in a single night, until one day, a deal was struck. They would offer willingly, on the same night each year, a first-born son to feed the spirit's hunger. And so it has come to pass that we offer our dearest Bogdan—a sacrifice so that others may live."

He could see her now among the crowd. A single tear glistened in the light of the moon as it rolled down her cheek. It comforted him, as he drew his final breaths, to know that she, at least, might grow old. If not beside her, he would live in her memories as a face that remained forever young.

Only a year before, he'd attended the previous sacrifice—another boy from another family. There was little mystery about what would happen next. In the morning, the villagers would return to collect his corpse, and it would be burned, along with his few possessions, upon the pyre. His name would be inscribed on a stone with the names of the others—the hundreds who had gone before him. And then he would be forgotten. Fields would be sown and crops harvested. Children would play and mothers would fret. The years would come and go the same way they'd come and gone since the beginning of time.

They left him there, tied fast to the tree and alone. He had waited his whole life for this moment. It was the waiting, he thought, that was the worst part.

He didn't have to wait long. No sooner than the priest and the last of the villagers had retreated to the shelter of their little homes, did a dark presence emerge from the forest. A scent filled his nose—death and decay and the rot of centuries. And as a shadowy hand wrapped itself around his throat, he saw a pair of eyes, burning red and bright, staring back at him through the night.

THREE

The autopsy report was woefully inconclusive. 'Natural death,' it read. It had not, as the investigator initially suspected, been a brain hemorrhage. The small amount of blood which had pooled on the floor beneath the poor woman was caused by nothing more remarkable than a self-inflicted bite to the tongue as she collapsed.

"It's just awful," said Nancy, as she discussed the matter with her husband. The nanny's next of kin had yet to be located. They'd packed her few things, the only items which remained to mark an otherwise unremarkable life, in a box which they'd placed beside the front door. It waited there, haunting them, a reminder of the unfortunate event which had occurred in their very expensive and otherwise perfect home.

Mr. Hardaway, for his part, seemed less bothered by what had happened than his wife. He was a busy man, after all. At the age of forty-five, he was already the CEO of a private equity firm, one of the largest in Boston, and indeed the entire East Coast. He openly suspected his wife's recent moodiness was less a product of sympathy than it was frustration, as she'd been left alone to care for Baby Nora until a suitable replacement could be found.

Nancy soon forget her troubles when the services of a particularly beautiful young nanny, a blonde-haired import from Sweden, became available. The nanny had come highly recommended by the Abernathy family, who—despite never having said such—everyone knew could no longer afford domestic assistance after Mr. Abernathy's creative investment practices fell under the scrutiny of the Securities and Exchange Commission. What wonderful luck it was for Mrs. Hardaway.

"I'm very happy you're here," she said, as she embraced her new nanny on the morning of her arrival. The cardboard box with the previous nanny's possessions, still waiting near the front door, wasn't enough to kill her spirits. "What's your name again, dear?"

"My name is Ingrid," said the new nanny with a lilting Swedish accent. "I'm sure you're already aware my dismissal from the Abernathy family wasn't due to poor performance."

"Yes, it's rather unfortunate. I've heard such dreadful things about those financial investigations." Once, she'd come home from a social function to find Mr. Hardaway in his study, feverishly feeding a box of documents into a shredder. It had only been a false alarm, he told her. There was nothing to worry about.

"Right this way," she said, leading Ingrid by the hand to the same room which had previously been occupied by their first nanny. "Inez—oh, Inez is our housekeeper—put a fresh change of sheets on the bed just this morning."

Ingrid smiled. "If you don't mind, might I ask why your previous nanny left?"

"Can I be frank, Ingrid?"

"We Swedes prefer frankness."

"Yes, well then, I'm quite certain you've heard the rumors. Boston is still, as they say, a small town."

Ingrid nodded as she placed her suitcase on the bed and surveyed the room.

"Right, well it was all a rather terrible incident. One moment she was fine and the next she'd collapsed. By the time they rushed her to the hospital, she was dead. Such a tragedy really."

"Oh, you must have been devastated."

"Truly."

"And the baby?"

"Hmm?" She was distracted by Ingrid's blue eyes—so pure and innocent.

"How's the baby?"

"Ah, she's fine." Baby Nora had survived the incident unscathed. In fact, she only seemed more radiant. Her skin, as Nancy had pointed out to her husband, was positively glowing. And much to her exhausted relief, Nora had been crying less since their previous nanny's untimely departure. Perhaps, Nancy thought to herself in her most private moments, the woman had simply been a terrible nanny.

With the details of her employment settled, Ingrid went at once to attend to the baby in the nursery. Nancy excused herself to her husband's study and filled a glass with Mr. Hardaway's finest single malt scotch. It was bad form, she knew, to drink during the day. But it was almost afternoon, and besides, after everything she'd been through, she thought she deserved a little relaxation.

That night, with Baby Nora sleeping soundly in her crib, Ingrid even offered to help Inez prepare dinner. The two women laughed and exchanged stories of home while Nancy helped herself to a second glass of scotch. At the dinner table, she smiled at Mr. Hardaway and wondered if things around the house might finally be improving. She was eager to return to her life as the socially well-connected wife of a successful Boston financier. Miss too many charity functions, she thought, and one of those upstart and dreadfully unfashionable housewives from the South End would swoop in to take your place. She wasn't about to sit idly by and let that happen.

Mr. Hardaway must have returned from work in an equally good mood, because that night in the bedroom he was frisky. After their romp, he'd drawn a hot bath for her, and she'd taken her usual sleeping pill with a third and final glass of her husband's scotch. She had no idea who'd invented the pills that ushered her to off to sleep night after night, but if it were possible she would have thanked them personally. How people had lived before such modern comforts, she couldn't fathom.

"How's work?" she asked her husband as they sat side-by-side in bed. She'd moved on from Vanity Fair to the latest Cosmo, a guilty pleasure, while he frowned over emails on his phone.

"Oh, fine. We're buying a new company—just a few more hiccups to get sorted—but it seems promising. How would you like a vacation home in Martha's Vineyard? Maybe we could even buy a boat. I've always wanted to learn how to sail."

"That promising?" She tried not to giggle while she imagined herself hosting the celebrities and well-heeled politicians who were known to summer on the exclusive island. "What do they do?"

"Hmm?" Mr. Hardaway pressed send—there was a cheerful little whooshing sound as the email departed for its destination.

"The company—what sort of business is it?"

"Oh, nothing terribly exciting. It's an investment vehicle, mostly for enormously wealthy Russians and Saudis who want to buy property. It's all a bit dull and straightforward, really."

"I see." She didn't pretend to understand what her husband did all day in his stylish downtown office. It's not that she wasn't smart, she'd graduated university at the top of her class, but rather that Mr. Hardaway volunteered so few details. It was better that way, he'd told her once when she'd pressed him for more information. She tried not to think too much about what he might have meant by that as she drifted off to sleep.

She couldn't be sure how long she had slept, only that the room was dark when she was woken by the shrill sound of Ingrid's screams. "Byron," she said, while poking her husband in the ribs. Her mind was immediately filled with the vision of their previous nanny, sprawled dead and bleeding on the nursery floor.

Her husband was already awake. He switched the lamp on and pulled his robe from the chair beside the bed. "Stay here. I'll go and see what happened."

And so she waited, expecting some kind of terrible news. What had she done, she asked herself, to deserve this? At least the baby wasn't crying. There was nothing more unnerving than the sound of her daughter's tears.

The door opened and her husband sat on the edge of the bed. He rubbed his tired eyes. "False alarm. It was only a terrible nightmare. Ingrid and the baby are fine."

"Thank goodness." She wanted to feel angry at the disturbance the new nanny had caused. After caring for Nora in the wake of their first nanny's death, she was in desperate need of beauty sleep. But she was too tired to feel angry. And there was something else, a deep, unsettling feeling that their troubles had somehow only just begun.

She tried to return to sleep, but sleep wouldn't come. It was far too late, she told herself, for another sleeping pill. She had things to do in the morning. A new dress had to be purchased for Friday night—the opening of a new art gallery featuring female African painters. She listened to her husband snore—he had always been a loud sleeper—and bemoaned her awful luck.

Ingrid brought her fresh squeezed juice and Swedish-style oatmeal in the morning. The young nanny was all apologies. She hadn't had a nightmare like that since she was a little girl. Perhaps it was just the unfamiliarity of a strange new room.

Nancy feigned graciousness. In truth, she was rather upset at the loss of her precious sleep, and wondered if the bags under her eyes had returned. "That's okay, dear," she said in her kindest tone. "These things happen. Would you like to come dress shopping with me this afternoon? Inez will be here to keep an eye on Nora."

"Oh, I couldn't abandon the baby on my first full day. It wouldn't be right of me."

Just as well. Nancy had always preferred to do her shopping alone.

She returned that evening fresh-faced and smiling. She'd found a wonderful floral number, she told her husband, with bright and vivid colors to match the art gallery's African theme. She'd even had time to visit the spa for a rescue treatment.

"There's nothing quite like a good facial," she said, as she described the fresh slices of chilled cucumbers they'd placed over her eyes, "to restore one's youthful vitality."

Inez, being of some kind of distant African descent, had even complimented her dress selection. And so she found herself in a generally favorable mood that night as she and Mr. Hardaway switched off their respective bedside lamps and drifted off to sleep.

She was woken again, sometime around three or four in the morning, by the sharp sound of Ingrid's bloodcurdling screams.

Her husband, despite being tired after another long day at the office, did the respectable thing and gathered himself up to go check on her. She was fine, he reported upon his return—it was just another nightmare.

When he finally climbed back into bed beside her, Nancy was in a less-than-charitable mood. "What are we going to do, Byron? I can't have that woman waking me up every night. This can't go on."

"Steady," he said. "It'll pass."

Only it didn't pass.

Despite the many and frequent apologies of the nanny, Nancy totally lost her patience on the third night, when she was woken again by the the horrible sound of the woman's screams.

"My dear Ingrid," she said, as they ate breakfast together in the sunroom adjacent the kitchen, "what are these nightmares that trouble you?"

Ingrid's face turned white. "I'd rather not say, Mrs. Hardaway. They're so unpleasant."

"Maybe talking about them would help." She'd already made up her mind to send Ingrid away if the nightmares didn't cease. The young Swede was certainly a wonderful nanny, of that there was little doubt. Nora had never seemed happier, and Nancy would mourn the loss of someone to care for her child. But the nightly interruptions had grown too much for her to bear.

"It's the draug, ma'am."

It was a word Nancy Hardaway was entirely unfamiliar with. "Draug?"

Ingrid's soft white face flushed bright red, as if she were terribly embarrassed. "An old Swedish myth. I've never believed in such things myself, but it's there each night in my dreams."

"I'm not sure I understand." She wondered if the girl might be crazy.

"The draug is an undead spirit, condemned to wander the earth. It comes in the night and feeds on the souls of the living. You wake suddenly, unable to breathe or move, with its crushing weight upon your chest. And the smell, such a terrible smell, like something has died and been left beneath the bed to rot."

Nancy thought it was rather ridiculous. Perhaps the girl was in need of serious professional help. "Has it happened before?"

"Ma'am?"

"This dream, is it normal?"

"No, ma'am. I should say once, when I was a little girl in Sweden, I awoke in the night with the same sensations. My grandmother had been telling us stories of the old days and I'm sure that was the cause. But it hasn't happened since, not until I arrived in your fine home. It's just—" The girl paused to collect herself. "—it feels so awfully real."

"I assure you, sweet Ingrid, you're quite safe here. Mr. Hardaway is careful to set the security alarm each night before bed, and the caretaker keeps a close eye on things from his basement apartment."

"Yes, ma'am." Ingrid let out a small, nervous laugh. "It's only a silly dream—nothing more. Please, Mrs. Hardaway, don't send me away. I adore your daughter and I'm sure it will pass."

After two more nights of dreadful screams, it was the nanny who packed her things and said goodbye to the Hardaway household. She was going back to Sweden, she told them, to recover from the experience.

Nancy, who'd felt guilty for wanting to send the girl away, found herself begging Ingrid to stay. But the girl was unmoved, and so for the second time in a matter of weeks she found herself without a nanny.

Later that night, as she sat in the nursery tending to Baby Nora, she remembered a time, years ago, when she'd wanted nothing more than to be a mother. It was, in fact, all she'd ever thought about. But Mr. Hardaway had been found insufficient, despite their many visits to the top fertility specialists in Boston. And so she'd resigned herself to the life of a social queen, until the day came when she could no longer imagine having a child.

Childbirth at thirty-six years old had not been easy. She was in labor for nearly seventeen hours, until the doctors insisted on an emergency cesarean section. Now, as she nursed Nora from a bottle, she wondered if maybe, just maybe, she still had a chance at becoming a good mother.

She put the bottle down on the table and slipped her shirt from her shoulder. Nora giggled as she raised her to her breast. This is what mothers do, Nancy thought. Tiny lips wrapped themselves around her nipple and a drop of warm milk ran down her chest. It was nice, the two of them sharing a moment.

As she cradled her baby another memory returned. She was reminded by something Ingrid had said—the story of the draug, an evil shadow in the night. Not long before she'd discovered she was pregnant, Nancy had awoken from her own nightmare.

She shivered now as she remembered the strange figure above her bed, the weight upon her chest as it enveloped her, squeezing the breath from her as she lay helpless, unable to move. Then it was gone, as quickly as it had come, and she found herself next to Mr. Hardaway, the sheets wet with sweat. Terrible morning sickness in the weeks after had sent her to the doctor, who'd confirmed she was with child. It was a miracle, they told her, considering her husband's shortcomings. But there, in the dimply lit space of the nursery, she couldn't help but wonder if things were somehow connected.

"Ouch," she said, as a sharp pain rose from her chest. When she looked down, there was a thin line of blood where the milk had run from her nipple.

Nora had bit her.

FOUR

"It's a miracle," said the priest. The villagers gathered around him in a half-circle at the edge of the village clearing—men and women with incredulous looks on their tired and worn faces. Only the small children laughed and played at their parent's feet, unaware of the significance of what they were witnessing.

For Bogdan, it was something like waking up from a long, fitful sleep. His head hurt, and his ears rang with a deafening thunder. He raised his hands to his face, wrists burned and sore from the twisting of the cords, to find little rivers of dried blood. And the sun—its morning rays bore into his eyes like the blade of a dagger. He'd never expected to see the sun again.

Thirst burned in his bone-dry throat, but the crowd was too busy discussing among themselves the implications of his survival to bother with bringing him water. It was a delicate voice, like something from one of the old songs, which parted the villagers and raised a wooden cup of water to his parched lips.

"Yekaterina," he said, drinking from the cup and taking her into his arms. "My love."

She was crying, much the same as the night before, only this time they were not tears of loss, but tears of joy.

That night, they gathered outside the house of the oldest and wisest man in the village to ponder what had happened. Some considered it a sign of good fortune, while others spoke only of doom.

"We're saved," said one of the men. "The beast has lost his power. He will trouble us no more."

"You're a fool," cried another. "The boy, for whatever reason we cannot yet say, has failed to honor the agreement. There will only be more death and blood to come."

Bogdan sat silently among them, wrapped in an animal skin with Yekaterina by his side. He'd spent the day with his family, his mother sobbing over him while his father sat stern-faced, gazing into the fire that burned in the hearth in the corner of their house. His brothers and sisters, never quite understanding what had happened or the true significance of the ceremony, had nonetheless been happy to see him, and offered hugs and kisses before retreating to play with their toys.

"My children," said the old priest who'd offered him up as a sacrifice to the evil spirit, "God has a plan. If only we might listen, he will reveal everything in due course."

The villagers wanted nothing of God's plan. They had grown restless, and the words of the priest did little to soothe their doubts. A call rang out among them to repeat the ceremony. It must have been a mistake, they said. He would be tied to the tree and offered again. It was the only way.

Bogdan said nothing. He was supposed to be dead, and though he found himself alive and well, something had changed deep inside him. He was no longer a boy without a future. He was a man, with the heavy weight of the world thrust suddenly upon his still-slender shoulders.

He was not the only one who had changed. Yekaterina, who'd sacrificed her love for the sake of the village, resembled little of the gentle girl with blue eyes who sang hymns and picked mushrooms in the forest. If he had become a man, so too had she become a women. He watched her listen to them now, debating his fate as though he was only something to be used and discarded. But they had forgotten that he was her husband and she his wife.

"Enough," she said, standing to address them as a mother might address her children. "My husband gave his life for you. He went eagerly to the tree of death and thrust himself upon it. He did not once complain. And he has returned to walk again among us."

The villagers fell silent—so silent one could hear the logs spark and crackle on the communal fire they'd built to warm the cool night. The only sound, save for the fire, was a baby crying somewhere in the distance.

"Have you not witnessed a true miracle?" Her blue eyes burned brightly in the light of the flames. "Is it not as the priest has said?"

Those who had spoken on his behalf nodded their heads in agreement.

A single voice of dissent rose from the back of the crowd. "But what of the spirit, good woman?"

"He has come," she said. "My husband has denied him."

"It's true," said another voice. "Bogdan has beaten the spirit who has plagued our people for centuries."

Their voices soon formed a chorus, men and women and even some of the children sounding his name, sending it up

into the starry sky on the sparks of the fire. "Bogdan! Bogdan! Bogdan!"

Still more voices joined in, until the entire village called
his name in steady unison.

Yekaterina raised her arms high above her head and
dropped them with a sudden violence. "Return now to your
homes. Tend to your fields and your families, and trouble
yourselves with the evil spirit no more, for he has been van-
quished from our lands by Bogdan—Bogdan the Great!"

And so Bogdan and Yekaterina found themselves alone
in the bed which had been prepared for the consummation
of their sacred marriage. She traced his skin with loving
hands, tended to the burns upon his wrists and pledged to
restore him.

"Kiss me, husband."

He did as she said, until they were joined together for a
second time in both body and spirit. When it was over, they
laid side-by-side, listening to the sounds of the night. A light
rain had fallen over everything. Gentle drops pattered
against the wooden planks of the roof.

"Tell me," she said, "what happened to you at the edge
of the forest?" She spoke plainly, without the boldness she'd
exhibited earlier in the night when she'd addressed the
crowd.

"I don't know."

"Surely, you must remember something."

"I remember a shadow, and the smell of death. There
were eyes—red as fire. And I remember invisible hands,
wrapping themselves tightly around my throat until I
couldn't breathe."

They'd called it a miracle, the priest and the villagers, but
in truth there was little he could remember about what had

happened. Everything had gone dark, and when he'd opened his eyes it was morning.

"And how did you save yourself?"

He thought about what she'd asked, struggling to recall something, anything, he might have done. But there was nothing. He shrugged his shoulders.

"No matter, husband." This time it was she who kissed him. "Maybe it was our love. Not even the darkest of spirits could come between us. Take me again, Bogdan the Great."

They made love once more on the heavy animal skins of the bed. And when they finished and he'd rested they did it again, continuing this way late into the night. It was true, what she'd said. He'd gone to die as a boy and returned a man, the only one among them who'd ever survived the evil spirit. His name would not be inscribed upon the rock with the others. A new monument would be erected—new tales would be told and new songs would be sung. And they'd remember him, Bogdan the Great, for all of eternity.

FIVE

The Hardaway's third nanny departed even faster than Ingrid had left. The poor girl had been so terrified she didn't even bother to collect her paycheck. She'd only mumbled incoherent words about ghosts and the Devil as she gathered her things and made a beeline for the front door—Nancy pleading with her all the while to stay.

Nancy was convinced they were cursed. Even Inez, who stayed with her family on the other side of the city and rode the train to work, had taken to burning candles imbued with images of saints and singing Christian hymnals as she worked around the house. The faithful woman had offered to bring a crucifix from her family's home to hang in the Hardaway's townhouse, but Nancy had politely declined. She wouldn't have any of her friends thinking she had become a Catholic.

That afternoon, after Inez had reluctantly agreed to keep an eye on Nora, she attended afternoon tea service in the elegant Reserve Lounge of the Langham Hotel with a particularly wealthy and well-connected social acquaintance.

She wore one of her favorite dresses, light blue, with a strand of white, freshwater pearls that framed her slender collarbones. But even her impeccably polished appearance, immaculate as it was, and for which she received numerous compliments from her companion, wasn't enough to lift her heavy spirits.

"I don't understand," she said. "We pay them quite well. Good help is just so hard to find these days."

"Don't be cliché, dear." Her friend, one Mrs. Johnson, was born into a family which had long come from money, and whose position at the upper echelon of Boston society was undisputed. As such, she enjoyed the luxury of speaking rather frankly. "We've all heard the rumors about the nightmares."

Nancy tried not to show her dismay. The high society families formed a tight circle, and if word had already circulated among the other nannies about their troubled home, it would make finding a suitable replacement next to impossible.

Mrs. Johnson leaned forward and whispered across the table. "What you need, Nancy, is to cleanse your home from whatever evil has taken up residence within your walls."

She knew, like everyone in Boston knew, that her friend had a penchant for the occult. Women with such extravagant means sometimes took an interest in rather bizarre things. It was to be expected—the product of an idle lifestyle. But Nancy had never been the type for religion, or superstition of any kind, though she dutifully attended St. Peter's Episcopal Church with her husband whenever social conventions required.

"I know a man," said her friend. "He's something of an exorcist. Perhaps he can help you."

"An exorcist?" It was absurd, of course, but she was reluctant to offend Mrs. Johnson. "Good heavens. Do you really think we need an exorcist?"

"Oh, he's just wonderful—cleans up all the messy energy that finds its way into the corners and attics of these dreary old homes. I'm certain he could help you. Do let me make arrangements for a session."

Under normal circumstances, Nancy would have politely declined the offer. But she was desperate for a stroke of good luck, and if playing along with the exorcist would endear her further to Mrs. Johnson, then perhaps it was worth inviting a little foolishness into her home.

She returned from her rendezvous buoyed by an unexpected streak of optimism, and made plans to share the idea with Mr. Hardaway that evening.

"Absolutely not," he said. "I'll not allow a stranger into my house to perform some kind of ritual. Have you lost your mind?"

"It's harmless," she said, as she poured them each a glass of scotch. "Mrs. Johnson was quite enthusiastic. Think of it as an opportunity to bring our two families closer."

It was the last thing she'd said which gave him pause. The Johnson's were positively loaded. Mr. Hardaway, never one to shirk a potential investor, found himself agreeing to the insane scheme if only for a chance to crack the Johnson family fortune.

"What a charming home you have, dear." Mrs. Johnson had arrived wearing head-to-toe white for the special occasion. "You simply must invite me over more often."

Charming. Nancy smiled. She knew quite well that what Mrs. Johnson had really meant was small, and while the Hardaway's historic townhouse was quite large compared to the average home, it must have seemed like a cottage in contrast to the Johnson's palatial estate. The high society ladies were always doing that—disguising an insult as a compliment. It was their way. But Nancy couldn't help but wonder why such wealthy women felt so insecure as to trade insults. "Thank you," she said. "Mr. Hardaway and I will be sure to invite you and your generous husband to our next event."

"Splendid." The woman fussed about while they waited for the man she'd said was an exorcist. "Might I trouble your housekeeper for a cup of coffee?"

"It's no trouble," said Nancy. She'd have to prepare the coffee herself. When Inez, with all her talk of superstitious old wives' tales and Jesus, had learned what sort of pseudo-witchcraft the two women were planning, she'd insisted on taking the afternoon off. Nancy could hardly blame her. It did seem rather strange to be hosting an exorcism with one of the wealthiest and most well-regarded women in Boston.

She'd just brought them each a coffee, along with an assortment of fine biscotti, when there was a heavy knock at the front door. Mrs. Johnson sprung from her seat. The woman seemed positively delighted. "That's him," she said. "He's a very busy man, dear. Don't keep him waiting."

Nancy was surprised by the appearance of her honored guest. He was shorter than she had imagined, with a bald head shaved clean and so well-polished it resembled a bowling ball. He wore a lopsided bow-tie, which gave him a frumpy appearance despite his perfectly pressed velvet suit. She invited him in at once, but the man insisted she inspect his business card.

It read: ALOICIOUS RUPERT THORNEWOOD, ESQUIRE. PARANORMAL INVESTIGATOR AND EXORCIST AT LARGE.

"Everything appears to be in order," she said. "Won't you come in, Mr. Thornewood?"

Convinced the proper formalities had been completed, he took one giant step across the threshold, and the three of them took up positions around the table in the breakfast room. Nancy brought another cup of coffee, to which he added three heaping spoons of sugar and stirred vigorously before taking the first sip.

"My dear Aloicious, how are you?" Mrs. Johnson addressed him with the sort of gushing manner with which one might address a celebrity.

"I'm quite well, thank you." His voice was thin and drawn, with a strange accent that sounded as though it was forced. "But I must say these are troubling times for Boston. Business has been rather brisk."

"Oh, good heavens," said Mrs. Johnson. "I hope we haven't imposed too much on your busy schedule."

The corners of his pursed lips turned up into something resembling a smile. "I'm never too busy for my favorite client."

The wealthy socialite blushed and busied herself with the coffee.

"Of course," he said, "there is the small matter of the payment."

Mrs. Johnson's knee bumped Nancy's leg beneath the table—a less-than-subtle reminder not to keep Mr. Thornewood waiting. Nancy took an envelope from her purse and slid it in front of the odd little man. "As you requested. Cash payment."

He thumbed through the notes and nodded with satisfaction. "Then it's settled. Why don't you tell me about what's been occurring?"

She recounted the story of losing three nannies in less than a month to what could only be described as the same terrible nightmare. He listened intently and took notes on a lined pad, which he'd produced from an old-fashioned leather bag of the sort doctors used to carry on house-calls.

When she'd finished, he was still scribbling notes in his little pad. "Yes, this is very concerning. It appears to be a classic case of haunting, Mrs. Hardaway."

"Haunting?"

"Indeed." The small man rubbed his smooth chin. "Fortunately, I've seen many of these cases before."

"He's been featured on GhostFinders," said Mrs. Johnson.

Aloicious Thornewood, if that was in fact his real name, smiled wide. "Nothing a simple exorcism won't clear up. Now if you'd be so kind as to show me the nanny's room."

Nancy led them both up the stairs and along the corridor, until they reached the simple room where all three nannies had slept. Baby Nora was taking her afternoon nap in the nursery just across the hall. She hoped the exorcism wouldn't be so loud as to wake her.

"Do you feel that?" Mr. Thornewood's deep-set eyes darted back and forth around the room. "I'm sensing a truly malevolent presence. Under normal circumstances, the fee I quoted would be insufficient to extract such evil. But since you're a friend of Mrs. Johnson, I'm prepared to make accommodations."

Nancy had the feeling he was putting on something of a show. "That's very generous."

The man in the velvet suit got to work at once, removing all manner of peculiar items from his leather bag and placing each one neatly on the bed. "A vial of salt from the Dead Sea," he explained, holding up a thin tube of glass. "A pressed thistle from the Scottish Highlands."

Mrs. Johnson seemed positively enthralled. Her enthusiasm climaxed when he produced a pentagram on a long silver chain and hung it around his neck. "What, might I ask, is that?"

"A gift," he said, "from the Sacred Order of the Gnostics of Byzantium—to guarantee the safety of my soul as I work to battle the evil spirits."

"Oh my, you really have come quite prepared, Mr. Thornewood."

"One can never be too prepared when battling evil, my dear Mrs. Johnson. Now if you'd both excuse me, I must be left alone to complete my task. I'm afraid what happens next isn't safe for the uninitiated."

"Yes, of course," said Mrs. Johnson.

They returned to the breakfast room, and Nancy poured them each another cup of coffee while they waited. "How long have you known Mr. Thornewood?"

"Good heavens, it's been years. He's such a wonderful man. I've consulted with him on a number of distressing matters."

Nancy could only imagine how much money Mrs. Johnson had given the odd little man over the years. She reconsidered leaving him alone so close to Nora's nursery.

An hour passed and they had just switched to tea—it was far too late in the day for any proper lady to be drinking coffee—when they heard Mr. Thornewood scream. It was a ghastly wail for such a small man, as if he'd actually seen a ghost. Nancy went to the staircase and was about to ascend when he came rushing down in a terrible fright—a genuine look of horror upon his weaselly little face.

"Get out," he said. "It's not safe for you to be here. This place—it's home to something truly evil. Pack your things and leave this house at once!"

Mrs. Johnson offered to fetch him a glass of water from the kitchen, but he went straight for the door. Like the Hardaway's previous nanny, he hadn't even bothered to gather his things.

Nancy wondered what he could have possibly seen that would have sent him into such a panic. "I thought you could help us."

"There's no helping you," he said. "Whatever evil lurks in this house is beyond even my most capable abilities." He took her by the arm and squeezed.

"Stop," she said. "You're hurting me."

"Get out! Get out while you still have a chance!" He released his grip and paused at the door only long enough to throw the envelope of money to the floor. Bills scattered and spread themselves on the black and white tiles.

Mrs. Johnson followed him out in a hurry, waving her arms about in every direction. "Mr. Thornewood! Oh, dear Mr. Thornewood, do come back!"

Upstairs in the nursery, Baby Nora was crying.

SIX

Fire burned all around him. The village he'd known his whole life was engulfed in flames. Wooden roofs sent ribbons of thick smoke up into the black night sky. Men raced in every direction with heavy buckets of water, a vain effort to contain the wild blaze. And the screams—everywhere there were screams.

"Can you help me?" It was a woman who'd cared for him as a child. Her face was badly burned. In her arms she carried the ashen corpse of a baby. "Please, he won't move. Can you help me?"

It was too late. He tried to make her understand, but the woman wouldn't listen. She clutched at his shirt with fingers blackened by flames. He broke free and wiped sooty sweat from his brow. Where was Yekaterina?

He raced from one burning house to another, the screams of the dying filling his ears as he went. He went to the house where her family lived and tried the door. The heat had left it warped and twisted. When he finally managed to yank it open, a cloud of smoke billowed out, followed by a young boy whose nightgown was entirely up in flames. The boy screamed and flailed about, clawing at his peeling skin in torturous agony.

"Yekaterina!" His heart beat in his chest. His eyes burned. He could never live without her. "Where are you, Yekaterina?"

"I'm here." Her voice cut through the violent cacophony of noise to reach his ears. "I'm here, my love."

But he couldn't see her. There was only the fire and the smoke and the sounds of the dying.

"I'm here," she said. "Open your eyes, Bogdan. Open your eyes."

He did as he was told, and he found himself beside her in their bed. His body was covered in sweat. The cool night air sent a shiver across his skin. "I've had the most terrible dream."

"Yes," she said. "You thrashed about wildly in your sleep."

He pulled her close and kissed her gently on the forehead. She looked so beautiful, smiling back at him now. She was his magic, and he swore to himself he would never lose her.

"Sleep, my love." She ran her fingers through his thick blonde hair and traced the shape of his neck. "When you wake again you'll find me still beside you."

He laid still for a long time, his mind filled with images of flames. The old ones said that every dream has a meaning, and he wondered what such a dream could possibly mean for him, for her, for the people of their village. It was only the sound of her gentle breath—in and out, in and out—that lulled him back to sleep. But peace is a fragile thing, and he was woken again by a heavy knock on the door.

"Stay here," he told her, as he slipped on his woven shirt and tucked a large hunting knife into his waistband.

It was one of the men of the village. "Please, Bogdan. You must come and help."

"What's happened?" Such interruptions had become a regular occurrence. The villagers had taken to calling on him for all manner of problems in the weeks that followed his miraculous survival.

"It's Kyrill," said the man, a worried look spreading across his face. "He went into the forest to forage for berries and hasn't returned. His mother is in hysterics. All the men of the village are out looking for him."

"How long has he been gone?"

"Eight, maybe nine hours. It's not like Kyrill to be gone for so long. He's only a boy."

Yekaterina stood behind him and placed her steadying hand on his shoulder. "Go, husband. The people need you. I'll be waiting for your safe return."

He gathered his things and lit an oil lamp, followed the man out into the darkness of the night.

The village had come to life in the early morning hours, as they searched every corner and hiding place. Even the children, many of them stirred awake by the noise of the men and women, stood in their nightgowns at the edge of the forest and called the boy's name.

Bogdan assembled their most skilled hunters and readied a search party. There was Svyatoslav with his hound, his son who was keen with a bow, and a half a dozen more rough men who knew the forest well. Each carried an oil lamp as they set out into the woods, the pale light shifting through the trees and throwing strange shadows in all directions as they advanced.

It wasn't long before the hound picked up a scent, his bark breaking the empty silence. They followed him through thick undergrowth and along a small stream, stopping only when one of the men found a strip of cloth tangled in a thorny bush.

Svyatoslav held it up to his lamp for inspection. "It's a piece of Kyrill's shirt."

Whether it was good news or cause for concern, Bogdan couldn't be sure. They continued along the stream for what seemed like an hour, the hound pausing occasionally to re-new the scent.

How much time had actually passed, no one could say. The forest had become so thick it was difficult to see the moon. Snarled branches closed in all around them, tugging at their clothes like the hands of invisible beasts. As the night wore on, Bogdan began to give up any hope of finding the boy alive.

Then, in a small clearing at the base of a gently sloping hill, they found Kyrill's thin and pale figure lying naked in the babbling waters of the shallow stream. Bogdan knelt down beside the boy, who in truth was not much younger than he, and listened for a breath.

The boy's face and lips were an alarming shade of blue, but as Bogdan leaned in closer he heard the faintest whisper, a tiny, raspy sliver of breath moving in and out of the boy's slender chest. "Quick," he said to Svyatoslav, "give me your cloak."

Their small party moved carefully, slowed by the weight of Kyrill's limp body, as they followed the stream back in the direction they had come. When one man grew tired of car-rying the boy, they passed him along to the next.

Day had nearly broken when they reached the village.

It was only there, in the hazy first light of dawn, before the night had fully given way to day, that Bogdan turned to look over his shoulder. Somewhere in the distance, between a tangled web of leaves and branches, a pair of glowing red eyes stared back at him.

Word spread quickly of their return. Those who had continued searching for the boy throughout the night were the first to assemble around them. It wasn't long before the whole of the village had gathered.

"Get back," said Bogdan, cradling Kyrill in his arms. "Someone light a fire. He needs a fire!"

"Kyrill!" The boy's mother screamed when she saw the poor state of him. She fell to the wet earth and pleaded for God to save her only son.

"Husband—" Yekaterina's face was steady and calm, an island in the chaos that swirled around her. "I've kept the fire burning in our house, for I had no doubt you would find him and bring him back to us."

And so they placed the boy before the warmth of the fire and covered his naked body in animal skins. Yekaterina sent his mother home. "You need sleep," she told the tired woman. "Rest and don't trouble yourself. I won't let anything happen to him."

She nursed young Kyrill for three full days—only stopping to sleep for an hour or two when Bogdan or one of the other women from the village insisted. On the fourth morning, the boy opened his eyes and spoke.

"Where am I?" The words moved slowly from his lips as he struggled to form each sound.

"You're safe," she told him, placing her hand on his forehead. "Rest easy now, for you are in the home of Bogdan the Great."

On the fifth day, the old priest, who'd been attending an annual religious gathering in a nearby settlement, came to the house and laid his blessings upon the boy. He traced holy water over Kyrill's forehead and made the sign of the cross, much the same as he'd done for Bogdan on the eve of the sacrifice. When he'd satisfied his priestly duties, the two men retired together to a rustic table beside the hearth.

"It doesn't make any sense, father." Bogdan rubbed his tired eyes. He'd slept little more than his faithful wife in the days since he'd returned with the search party. "It's not like Kyrill to take such a risk. How could the boy have wandered alone so far from the village?"

The priest stroked his grey beard. "How could you have survived the night of the ceremony? Sometimes, my son, it's not for men to understand the will of God."

"There's something else, father. Something that's been troubling me as I lay awake."

"Yes, my son?"

He'd said nothing of the red eyes to anyone, not even his precious Yekaterina. He'd hoped, in those private moments when he allowed his mind to wander, that it had been nothing more than his imagination—a ray of early morning light reflecting in some strange way to mark the dawn. But his silence had grown heavy, until he could bear it no longer. "I saw something, father—something which I hoped never to see again."

The priest nodded. "We've all seen a great many things in recent days—not least of all the miracle of your very existence."

"This was no miracle. It was the evil spirit. He was out there in the forest that night, stalking us through the dark. I fear he has returned to take vengeance."

"You denied him once, Bogdan the Great." The old man took Bogdan's hands and held them between his own. "You shall deny him again."

Bogdan lowered his head and sighed. The long days and nights with young Kyrill in the house had left him exhausted. "Then it's true—our troubles are far from over."

The priest only smiled. "Our troubles are never over, my son, not until we rest in the house of the Lord."

On the sixth day, the boy had the strength to sit upright. He ate heartily the soup which Yekaterina brought him. His mother, who'd taken to spending the days locked away inside her house, was overjoyed when she came to see him.

The villagers called it another miracle—the second they'd witnessed in only a month. Theirs was truly a blessed village. People would surely come from miles around to pray in their simple church and receive counsel from the man called Bogdan the Great.

When the boy had recovered sufficiently, Bogdan took a seat beside him on the animal skins and asked if he remembered anything of what had happened that night in the forest.

"Even now it seems like a dream. I went to pick fresh berries for dinner. My mother loves fresh berries, and I know all of the best places to find them. I'd just filled my basket when I heard a strange voice call my name from deep within the woods. I thought it might be my little sister calling for help—she often trails behind me despite the protests of my mother—so I followed it along the creek. The last thing I remember was tripping over the root of a tree and tumbling into the water. When I next opened my eyes I was beside your fire."

"Did you see anything?"

Kyrill shook his head. "I'm sorry, Bogdan. That's all I can remember."

"Let him rest, dear husband." Yekaterina appeared in the doorway with a basket of vegetables. "Our handsome Kyrill must save his strength for the girls of the village. It seems they have been quite preoccupied with the state of his health." She smiled over her shoulder as she busied herself with potatoes and onions. "And save your own strength, Bogdan the Great. I'm in need of your gentle touch tonight."

On the seventh day, young Kyrill was strong enough to return home. That night, a great feast was held to honor the men of the search party. The whole of the village had come to celebrate in triumphant spirit.

Bogdan wasn't in the mood for celebration. He scanned the edge of the forest, half expecting to see a glowing pair of red eyes staring back at him. But there was only darkness.

Yekaterina, seated beside him, placed her soft hand over his. "Something eats away at you, husband. I can see it on your face."

He feigned a smile. "It's nothing, my love. I'm only tired."

"Don't lie to me, Bogdan the Great. You watch and wait. Who do you expect to see?"

He thought about telling her, but it wasn't the right time or place. Let them be happy, he thought, at least for the night. Who could say what tomorrow would bring?

Svyatoslav, already on his fourth or fifth beer, raised his tankard in the air and steadied himself against the table. "My friends, I propose a toast to our good fortunes. Bogdan the Great has defeated the evil spirit, and our handsome pup Kyrill has been returned safe into his mother's arms—much to the satisfaction and delight of the many fine girls of our village!"

A quiet laughter rose among them.

He took a hearty swig of beer and continued. "May the harvest be bountiful and may our bellies remain full through the winter!"

At this, they erupted into a collective cheer. Somewhere at the edge of their little gathering, a musician commenced an old folk song on a stringed instrument. The men danced in a circle, hands together and raised above their heads, while the women laughed at those unfortunate enough to miss a step. They carried on this way until late in the night, drinking and dancing and celebrating the luck that had visited their village. Even the old men, who'd lived through far worse times, seemed happy and joyful. It wasn't until the early morning hours when the last of them stumbled back to their little houses to sleep off the night's festivities.

Bogdan, as always, was joined by his lovely Yekaterina. Her ever-present hand, so delicate and beautiful, found its way to his shoulder and began to unbutton his shirt. "Make love to me," she said. "Make sweet love to me, my handsome prince."

Maybe that's what he was—a prince. The son of poor peasants, whose only lot in life was to be marked for death, he'd risen from the ashes and returned a leader of men. Perhaps it was as the priest had said. He'd defeated the evil spirit once before, even if he was unsure of the manner by which he'd accomplished such a feat. Perhaps, should the need arise, he could do it once more.

He took her again that night, their warm bodies twisting and bending in the flickering light of the fire, two parts of a single whole.

"Bogdan," she said.

"Yes, my dear?"

"Tell me you will love me forever."

He kissed her tender lips. "I will love you forever, Yekaterina. There will never be another—there could never be another as beautiful as you."

And there, before the fire and joined as one, they achieved perfect ecstasy—a single moment so present and pure, not even the terrible ravages of time or death itself could destroy it.

When they'd finished, she stroked his cheek with the back of her slender fingers. "I wish to know what disturbs your thoughts. You must unburden yourself to me, or it will set wrinkles to your face."

"In the forest, the night we returned with the boy, I saw the evil spirit."

"Then it's as I thought, for only such a vile and evil thing could worry my husband. But do not trouble yourself, my love, for you are the only one who has ever seen the beast and lived."

He wondered if what she had said was true. If it was as he suspected, then young Kyrill had also received a visit from the evil spirit while gathering berries in the forest. The boy had paid a terrible price, and might have died like the others were it not for his intervention, yet still he lived.

"Very well," he said. "I shall not worry. Should the spirit return I will defeat him again, once and for all."

"Yes." She returned his kiss. "You are truly a man now, dear husband, for I am with child, and you shall be a father."

SEVEN

It was exactly as she'd feared. Word of their troubled home spread quickly through the finer houses of Boston, and finding another nanny was proving to be impossible. Her friends, once eager to join her for afternoon tea or a glass of wine on the verandah, had taken to avoiding the Hardaway place as though it were, in fact, the subject of some ancient and terrible curse. Even Mrs. Johnson had been avoiding her after the failed exorcism and sudden flight of Mr. Thornewood.

With nobody to watch baby Nora, Nancy's lack of attendance at recent social functions had not gone unnoticed. She imagined what they might whisper in her absence— ripened women trading secrets in the powder rooms of Boston's most exclusive restaurants and hotels.

Things only became worse when Mr. Hardaway, whose work demands already required extensive travel, began to take longer and more frequent trips to such exotic places as Panama, Switzerland, and the United Arab Emirates. She loathed him while he was away, and on the occasions when he returned, spent a great deal of time sniffing his clothes in search of any unusual womanly scents.

Once, after a particularly long trip to some unspecified location in Europe, she'd found a balled up napkin in his pocket with a strange phone number scribbled in blue ink. When she called the number, it rang and rang with no answer. Mr. Hardaway, who'd explained many times his reasons for keeping the details of his work a secret from his wife, refused to answer any of her questions. In a moment of uncontrollable rage, she threw a book at him, the latest Danielle Steel hardcover, and they'd both gone to sleep in separate quarters—she in the bedroom and he on the leather sofa in the study.

He returned from his most recent trip overseas to find her alone and terribly exhausted. Distraught and rather teary eyed, she'd sent faithful Inez home early before taking up position on the sofa where he'd spent the night only a week before. She helped herself again to his spirits, this time a fine aged cognac imported from France, and made no offer to pour him a glass.

"I'm worried about you, Nancy." He sat beside her on the sofa and reached out with a hand.

She pulled away. "You don't seem very worried. You're gone so often I'd be surprised if you gave much thought to me or what goes on in this house."

"That's not fair, Nance. I'm providing for you and the baby. How do you think we can afford this house?"

He hadn't called her Nance since the early days when they'd first met. He was so handsome back then—an ambitious young man staking his claim. He'd pursued her with the kind of chivalrous enthusiasm she'd only read about in books.

"I hate it." She emptied the last of the cognac from her glass and poured herself another. "I hate this house, Byron. It's dark and drafty and empty. Do you remember the parties we used to host—the wonderful parties?"

"Of course," he said. "It wasn't so long ago. How could I forget the time Mrs. Montgomery drank too much champagne and fell into the goldfish pond?"

Nancy almost laughed. "She was wearing that ridiculous dress, the one she'd brought back from Paris. She wouldn't shut up about how much that hideous thing had cost. We were all so glad to see it ruined."

Mr. Hardaway filled his own glass. "I know it's tough on you, Nance—all of the traveling. Things will settle down and go back to normal. You'll see."

The smile left her face. "I'm tired, Byron. I'm so terribly tired."

"I know, honey."

Upstairs in the nursery, Baby Nora began to cry. Nancy, upon hearing the baby's tears, couldn't help but cry along with her. Big, wet tears rolled down her cheeks as she buried her worn face in her hands. "Heaven help me! Will I never rest?"

"Stay here," said her husband. "Have another cognac. I'll check on the baby."

She was too tired to argue with him, and relieved to finally have some help with the baby, even if only for a short time. She wondered if she'd ever attend lavish parties again, or lunch with friends, or spend her husband's money in her favorite boutiques on Newberry Street.

When Mr. Hardaway returned, he was glowing with the sort of pride all new fathers have for their first child. "She's really quite beautiful," he said. "Are you breastfeeding again?

Nora's put on weight in the last few weeks—she's strong and healthy."

Nancy had been too exhausted to notice. "Sometimes I wish she'd never been born."

It was a slip of her tongue, something she never would have said under normal circumstances. The weeks and months had been gnawing at her sense of decency, and though she regretted having such thoughts about her own baby, it felt good to say it aloud. Something inside of her, some pressure which had been building, was suddenly released. She relaxed into the sofa and took another sip of her husband's expensive cognac.

"You can't mean that, Nancy. She's our child."

Now that it had been said, she couldn't possibly take it back. Besides, she was never one for serious regrets. "I liked things better when it was just the two of us."

"But you always wanted a child. You were devastated when the doctors said my chances were slim."

He was right. She had wanted a child. After their many trips to the fertility specialists had come up fruitless, she'd spent months in therapy working through her disappointment, until she finally gave up hope of ever becoming a mother. But that was years ago, when she was younger and full of life. Nora had left her entirely depleted.

He returned to his place beside her on the leather sofa and put a hand on her knee. "We'll find another nanny. I promise."

"It doesn't matter," she said. "They all run away."

"Then we'll find another. David Hirschbach—you remember his lovely wife Evelyn—told me about an agency that recruits French nannies from Europe. Wouldn't that be wonderful? Nora could learn to speak French."

"You promise?" She tried to imagine how jealous the other women would be of a French nanny.

"Anything for you."

Whatever tiny sliver of hope she might have felt soon vanished when the baby began to cry again. Her husband disappeared and she sat alone, wallowing in her terrible fortune. Mr. Hardaway had just returned and was pouring himself another glass when there was a peculiar knock on the front door.

"It's late," he said. "Who could it be?"

The old grandfather clock in the corner of his study sprung to life as if on cue. It was exactly midnight.

An old woman, face wrinkled and grooved, waited on the front porch. Despite the worn features of her face, she stood completely straight, her broad shoulders filling the space beyond the doorway. A thin wisp of gray hair protruded from the embroidered scarf tied tightly beneath her chin. In her hands, she clutched a scratched and faded leather bag, not at all dissimilar to the bag that weaselly little huckster Mr. Thornewood had carried. Nancy wondered what the old woman might be selling at such a late hour.

"Yes?" said Mr. Hardaway. "Can we help you with something?"

The old woman's eyes sparkled a bright blue. "I've heard you're in need of a nanny." She spoke in a peculiar accent. The words bounced and drew out in long syllables as though she might be singing a song.

"Well," he said, "we are considering possible candidates, though I'm afraid at this hour I'll have to ask you to return at a more suitable time."

Nancy wasn't interested in waiting, and she knew as well as her husband that there were no other candidates. Besides, what harm could an old woman possibly be? "I apologize for my husband. Would you like to come in for a cup of coffee? It must be chilly in the night air."

The old woman smiled back at her, eyes still shimmering bright blue as she crossed the threshold and followed them both into Mr. Hardaway's study. "What a lovely home you have."

If she only knew, Nancy thought. Of course, she would say nothing of the curse. Perhaps the old woman would prove more resistant to nightmares. "I'm sorry," she said. "I'm afraid I didn't get your name."

"Iryna," said the old woman.

"Oh, how lovely." She sent Mr. Hardaway to fetch them each a cup of coffee. "Is that French?"

"Ukrainian."

"I see." She couldn't recall ever meeting a Ukrainian, and wondered if they had a reputation for making good nannies. "Forgive me, I couldn't place your accent."

The old woman was still smiling. "That's quite alright, dear. In truth, I was raised in Newfoundland, where my family has been settled for some time. My grandmother spoke Ukrainian in the home, while I spoke English in school with the rest of the children. It's understandable you would find my accent difficult to place."

She couldn't have said what it was, but there was something about the old woman that put her at ease. "Do you have experience with children?"

"Oh, yes," said Iryna. "I've been caring for children since my mother and father died. I was the oldest of seven, you see. It was only natural that I became a nanny, a capacity in which I have forty-six years of professional experience. I'm happy to provide references upon request."

It seemed too good to be true, that Iryna would arrive on their doorstep in her greatest moment of need. Mr. Hardaway had just returned with the coffee when the old woman asked if she might see the baby.

"I'm afraid she's sleeping," he said. "If you'd be so kind as to leave your contact details, we'll be in touch should we desire your services."

Nancy hoped the woman wouldn't be put off by her husband's cold reception, but Iryna only continued smiling as she added sugar to her coffee and stirred.

"Of course," said the woman. "You're quite right. Let sleeping babes sleep."

They were together in bed, and would have been side-by-side were it not for the large expanse of empty mattress between them. Mr. Hardaway sent the last of his nightly emails while Nancy examined the résumé left behind by the old woman.

"It's quite complete," she told her husband. "It says here she held her last position for ten years. I really do hope you'd consider inviting her back."

"Don't you think it's odd?" Mr. Hardaway placed his wire-rimmed reading glasses on the nightstand.

"Odd?"

"Well, yes," he said. "How many nannies go around knocking on doors at midnight?"

Nancy, who'd given up all hope of returning to her former life as the days and weeks with Baby Nora dragged on, couldn't imagine there was anything odd about it. In fact, the woman's sudden arrival had seemed to her like a wonderful stroke of luck. She was certain things would be different this time—that somehow the old woman would be the answer to all her hopeless prayers.

Her husband was less than convinced. "How did she even know we need a nanny?"

"Everyone in Boston knows we need a nanny, Byron. It's all those women can flap their gums about. I swear, they take special pleasure in my suffering."

"Well, I don't like it. Something about her gave me the chills."

Nancy had grown tired of her husband's endless skepticism and paranoia. "Frankly, I don't much care how you feel about the matter. You're not the one stuck in this house day after day with nothing to do but go crazy. I'm calling her tomorrow."

"Nancy—"

"Don't do that!"

"What?"

"Talk down to me. You're always talking down to me. It's easy for you—off traveling the world and doing God knows what while your wife stays home to play the good mother. It's my decision as the woman of this house, and I'm going to invite her back to meet the baby."

Mr. Hardaway sighed and rubbed his eyes. "Would you at least call to check her references?"

It was over. She had won. In truth, she was surprised he'd capitulated so easily. But she could be very insistent when she wanted something, and her husband was never the type to continue an argument before bed. "Of course," she said.

"Good. I love you both, Nancy. I only want you and the baby to be happy."

That night, as she drifted off to sleep with the steady hum of Mr. Hardaway snoring beside her, she was visited by a dream of her own. But it wasn't the same nightmare which had befallen the others. Instead, she dreamed of boutiques and banquet halls and luncheons. She wore her finest attire. And the high society ladies, so quick to overlook the things they'd whispered in her absence, welcomed her back with gushing compliments and open arms.

EIGHT

He was nudged awake by his wife in the early hours of the morning. He could see she was not well. Beads of sweat gathered on her face and reflected the orange glow of the slowly dying fire in the hearth. The animal skins beneath her were wet.

"Fetch the midwife," she said. "It's time."

He pulled a heavy cloak around his shoulders and set out into the cold night. It had been months since winter first arrived in the village. Still, the baby wasn't due for six more weeks. As he trudged through thick snow to a small house on the far side of the village clearing, Bogdan was filled with worry for the baby's health, and for the health of his beloved wife.

The windows of the house were dark. A heavy silence, the kind of silence which can only be found in the longest months of winter, had fallen over everything, save the ever-present sound of pine trees rubbing together at the edge of the forest. He took one last breath of the still night air and raised a fist to the door.

It was some time before he heard a commotion coming from inside. A lantern was lit—its light fell from the window and onto the snow.

"Who's there?" It was the voice of Svyatoslav, whose wife's tender and skillful hands had greeted nearly all of the children of the village. Even Bogdan, who was born destined for an early death, was coaxed from his mother's womb by her loving touch.

"It's me," he said. "It's Bogdan."

The door creaked open on its hinges, and Svyatoslav ushered him in from the cold. "What's happened, dear friend?"

"The baby—it's coming."

Svyatoslav rousted his wife from her sleep, and the house came alive with the busy gathering of things—herbs and linen and small glass vials of tinctures—before the three of them set off together into the snowy night.

They found her on the floor beside the bed. A patch of slick, crimson red had stained her nightgown where it rested between her legs.

"Help me," said the midwife.

The men eased Yekaterina back onto the bed and Svyatoslav's wife brought one of her tiny glass vials to the trembling woman's lips.

"Drink," she said. "It will ease the pain."

An hour passed, then another. Svyatoslav fed logs into the fire as his wife busied herself with boiling linens and preparing herbs.

Bogdan paced before the hearth, his thoughts interrupted only by the sound of Yekaterina's moans and screams. Once, when he was a boy, just twelve or thirteen, he'd helped his mother and the midwife tend to another woman in the village. They'd set him about to small tasks, gathering items they needed and tending to the fire. He'd stayed with them throughout the night, listening as they spoke among themselves in hushed whispers. In the morning, when the baby finally emerged, it was without breath. The poor mother, crying and sobbing, clutched her dead baby tightly in her arms and refused to let them take it away. There had been blood then, too.

"Come." Svyatoslav placed a rough hand on his shoulder. "Let the women do their work."

Bogdan followed him outside and they passed a pipe back and forth. The smoke was thick and harsh and burned his throat.

"She's bleeding too much," he said.

Svyatoslav loaded more of the dried herb into the pipe. "My wife is the best midwife on this side of the Carpathian Mountains. She'll do what she can."

He found little comfort in his friend's words. As the first hint of dawn broke over the horizon, the most blessed man in the village asked God for one more favor.

He hoped it wasn't too much to ask.

It was all a great mess of blood and sweat and terrible screams carrying up into the rafters of the house.

"You can do it," said the midwife. "Just one more push."

Yekaterina screamed wildly and squeezed his hand so tightly he thought she might break his bones.

Just when he thought she could push no further, the crown of a tiny head appeared between her legs. Svyatoslav's wife, with her experienced hands, was there to receive it.

"Again," she said. "Push again."

Once more, she squeezed his hand and screamed. He'd seen a great deal of things in his short life, but none so terrifying as childbirth. Even the evil spirit, with its red eyes and deadly grip, was no match for the ferocity of nature.

And then, as if the final culmination of some great effort, the baby suddenly slid free. It made no sound, and Bogdan couldn't be sure if it was alive or dead. The only thing he could be sure of, as the midwife cut the cord and spirited the baby away, was that his wife had lost a great deal of blood—too much blood for any one person to lose.

She managed a weak smile and clutched his hand with whatever remained of her strength. "Do you remember, my sweet husband, what I told you on the night of our wedding?"

Even in her wretched state she was the most beautiful thing he'd ever seen. He'd known, since the very moment they took him down from the tree still breathing, that it was her love that had saved him.

Heavy tears formed in his eyes and rolled in rivers of sadness down his face. "Please, I don't want to lose you."

"You can never lose me," she said. "I'm yours forever."

And then she was gone.

Somewhere in the room behind him, a baby cried.

"It's a boy," said the midwife. "A beautiful baby boy."

It took most of the morning to cut a path through the deep snow. The frozen earth required more effort, and they'd resorted to pickaxes, he and Svyatoslav working together, to finish digging the grave.

When the hole was dug, his friend left him alone in the fading hour of twilight. The priest had offered to come and say some words, but he thought it was only right that he should be alone with her one last time. Her family had said their goodbyes that afternoon, as she lay wrapped in white linen in the house that had been their home.

She was beside him now, resting on a bed of snow. He wiped a tear from his eye, and in the last light of day he lowered her into the hole. There were no flowers. No songs. There was only the emptiness of a broken dream—something that was gone forever and would never return.

The sky had grown dark by the time he finished replacing the earth. Above the place where her head rested, he planted a simple cross fashioned from two sticks. It was all that remained to mark her life—that and the son which he was left to raise alone.

"I promise," he said to her, "he'll be a good son, and the bravest of men." It was what she would have wanted.

He stood in the cold for a long while, gathering the strength to leave her. It was only when he turned to head back that a strange movement in the forest caught his attention.

"What do you want?" The words left his mouth in a fit of rage. "Is it my life you so desire? For I would gladly offer it that she might live again."

But the shadow said nothing. There were only those familiar red eyes, piercing deep into his soul through the darkness.

And then, for the second time in one day, he found himself completely alone.

NINE

Nancy sat at her husband's desk and examined the old woman's résumé. She was experienced, of that there was no doubt. Mr. Hardaway had insisted she check her references, but Nancy imagined there was no need. What harm could possibly come from such a kindly old woman? Her husband was simply being paranoid. It was one of his less desirable personality traits—a consequence of managing so much money.

She was about to dial the nanny from the desk phone when her cellphone rang. The screen lit up with a round picture of her husband. He'd have to wait. She pressed the 'ignore' button and had just gone back to the résumé when the phone rang again.

It was unlike Byron to call twice. Usually, it was she who rang him more than once when she needed something. He was always so busy with meetings.

"Yes?" She hoped whatever it was he would make it quick. She had plans to go shopping just as soon as the new nanny arrived.

"Listen carefully, Nancy." Her husband's voice was breathless, as though he was in a great hurry. "We don't have a lot of time. I need you to call Mr. Fellowes."

It was a signal they'd rehearsed many times, laughing with each over scotch or gin and tonic in the study. Mr. Fellowes was the name they'd given to her husband's shredder, and while she'd enjoyed the luxury of remaining ignorant to the specifics of her husband's work, she knew without a doubt what he was asking. She was no longer in the mood for laughing.

"Mr. Fellowes?" She couldn't believe it was actually happening. The day she'd always feared had finally come. "Are you sure?"

"Nancy—I love you."

Before she could reply, there was the sound of men on the other end of the line. They were taking her husband into custody, and it would only be a short while before they descended on the house.

There was no time for imagining what the neighbors might think. She sprung to life, bolting up the stairs in a rush to retrieve a key from a dummy can of shaving cream in the master bathroom.

Inez was waiting for her at the bottom of the stairs. "Is everything okay, Mrs. Hardaway?"

"Men and women will arrive soon," she said. She was surprised by the strength of her own resolve in such a stressful moment. "They're agents, Inez—agents from the federal government."

"Oh, dear."

They'd never found the need to concern their housekeeper with the complexities of Mr. Hardaway's business dealings, though it was clear from the expression on Inez's face she understood exactly what Nancy meant. "Whatever happens, I need you to look after Nora."

"Yes, ma'am. What should I do now?"

"I don't know," she said. "The same thing you always do."

She sprinted to the study and threw herself down on the floor, her hand trembling as she unlocked the bottom drawer of a file cabinet. Inside, she found a small safe with an electronic keypad and entered the code. She'd argued with him about making it so easy for anyone to guess, but now, with the clock ticking, she was glad she only had to remember her birthday.

Outside, on the narrow street in front of the Hardaway's townhouse, there were the sounds of vehicles screeching to a stop, doors opening and closing and the coordinated activities of half a dozen federal agents. Just enough time, she thought, to switch on Mr. Fellowes and shred whatever secrets her husband's documents contained. At least he wasn't stupid enough to keep them on the computer.

She fed the pages, one at a time, into the mouth of the machine and watched as line after line of account numbers were transformed into small pieces of confetti. If only the federal agents weren't already knocking at the front door, she would have burned the cross-cut shreds of paper in the fireplace. But it was too late. She took a final breath and composed herself.

"Mrs. Hardaway?" The man at the front door wore a navy blue windbreaker with 'AGENT' printed on the chest in big gold letters.

"Yes, that's me."

"I'm Special Agent Monroe with the Federal Bureau of Investigation. I have a warrant, signed by a judge, to search the premises." He held up an official looking document, complete with an original stamp, and passed her a black and white photocopy.

"Very well," she said. "Would you like some coffee while you work? Inez was just preparing a fresh pot."

The number rang for a long time before a sweet voice picked up on the other end. "Good morning. You've reached the law offices of Anthony J. Bennett. How may I direct your call?"

"I'm trying to reach Mr. Bennett," she said. "Please tell him it's an emergency."

"I'm sorry. Mr. Bennett is currently away from the office. Can I take a message?"

"This is Nancy Hardaway. I'm calling on behalf of my husband. Mr. Bennett should be expecting me."

The voice on the other end shifted into a deeper tone. "Of course, Mrs. Hardaway. Please hold a moment while I connect you."

She stayed on the line for what seemed like an hour while her call was connected to the lawyer's cellphone.

"Hello? Yes. I've been expecting your call, Nancy." The man spoke in short bursts as if his thoughts were occupied with several things at once.

"They're here," she said. "Agents from the Federal Bureau of Investigation."

"Hmm. That was quicker than I'd hoped. Were you prepared for their arrival?"

She knew he couldn't ask directly if she'd shredded her husband's documents. The government had a warrant, and one could never be sure who might be listening. But she was smart enough to take the hint. "Yes, Anthony. I was prepared. They're helping themselves to my coffee while they ransack Byron's study."

The man on the other end of the phone released a long sigh of relief. "You're a saint, Nancy—a real angel. I'm on my way to Byron as we speak."

"Is he okay? These bastards won't tell me anything."

"It's better that way," he said. "We don't want them thinking you know something. If they ask any questions, tell them you won't speak without your lawyer present."

"Yes, of course. But where are they taking him? We only had a moment before the call was disconnected."

"He's being booked at the county jail, Nancy."

Jail.

The word hit her hard. She imagined her poor husband stuffed into the back of some agent's car. It was a small relief they'd come for him at the office. At least the neighbors, who would surely be peering through their windows at the black vans parked in front of the house, wouldn't have the satisfaction of seeing Byron led away in handcuffs. "When can I see him?"

"Not today, I'm afraid. They'll take their time booking him and trying to conduct interviews. But don't worry, Nancy. I'll be with him and I won't let anything happen. Try to relax."

How was she supposed to relax while agents tore apart her house? She was afraid to ask the question that weighed on her mind. "And when—when will he be coming home?"

"They'll hold a preliminary hearing in a couple of days, and the judge will set bail. He should be home by the end of the week." The lawyer paused and sighed again. "But Nancy, these things can be complicated. Believe me, I'll do my best."

"Yes," she said, "that's what we pay you for."

From her place in the kitchen, she heard Baby Nora begin to cry upstairs in the nursery. One of the agents must have disturbed her. "Anthony," she said, "I have to go. It's the baby."

"Of course. Please trust me, Nancy. Your husband is in good hands."

She hung up the phone and climbed the stairs to where Nora had been sleeping. There was an agent beside the crib, rummaging around through a small cabinet while the baby kicked and wailed. Did these people have no sense of human decency?

"What do you think you're doing?"

"I'm sorry, ma'am. Our orders were very clear. We need to search everything."

"There's nothing in here but stuff for the baby." She took Nora in her arms and soothed her. She was surprised to feel such motherly instinct. Perhaps in moments like these, she thought, we have no choice but to become better versions of ourselves.

The agent gave her a flat smile and went back to his work. "You wouldn't believe where people hide things."

She took up position in a wicker chair in one corner of the nursery, Nora cradled in her arms, and waited for the brave men and women of the Federal Bureau of Investigation to finish their dispassionate work. She found some comfort in the baby's presence. Maybe it was love, or maybe the needs of her child gave her something to think about other than herself. Either way, she couldn't help but notice how beautiful Nora had become. It was as if she was seeing her for the first time since they'd brought her home from the hospital.

If only Byron could see us now, she thought. He'd be so happy. But Byron was on his way to jail.

The house was a disaster. Inez went from room to room in a fevered pitch, a desperate attempt to return some semblance of order. Nancy sipped tea on a stool at the kitchen counter. Her thoughts were cloudy—it was as if her whole body and mind had gone very numb.

"I can stay late," said Inez. "My sister can watch the kids tonight. I'd hate to leave you alone in this big old house."

"No, dear. You've been so wonderful." Nancy fumbled through her wallet for a few bills and pressed them into Inez's hand. "Skip the train tonight and call a taxi. The kids will be happy to see you."

"Yes, ma'am. Thank you. Now don't you worry about the house, Mrs. Hardaway. I'll come back first thing in the morning and we'll get everything cleaned up and put back in place. You'll see."

The woman was so kind, but Nancy wondered if it even mattered. She couldn't imagine they'd be hosting parties anytime soon. "Thank you, Inez."

A taxi arrived shortly to whisk the Hardaway's loyal housekeeper back to her waiting family. Baby Nora slept peacefully upstairs while Nancy sat alone in the kitchen, pots and pans still strewn on the floor around her.

She would have to take control now. Byron was in jail, and in the weeks and months that followed he'd be preoccupied with his legal defense. It fell on her shoulders to make decisions for the family, and her first decision was to hire the nanny.

The line rang and connected.

"Hello?" The old woman's voice, with its peculiar accent, felt immediately familiar.

"It's Nancy," she said. "Nancy Hardaway."

"Oh, wonderful. I was hoping you might call. I'd considered stopping by again but I didn't want to be a bother."

"Then your services are still available?"

"Of course, dear."

Byron wouldn't approve. But what did it matter what her husband thought? Everything had changed in a matter of hours, and Nancy would be left to pick up the pieces. She wasn't planning on doing it alone.

"Great," she said. "Can you be here in the morning?"

"How about eight o'clock?"

"Better make it nine." She'd never been one for early mornings. "Do you remember the address?"

"Yes, my dear," said the old woman. "How could I forget?"

TEN

The harvest had been bountiful. Their bellies remained full throughout the long winter and they had much cause to celebrate the arrival of spring. But there was no celebration in the village. Yekaterina's death still hung in the air, and they went about their business in silent mourning.

Bogdan stood before her grave and wept. Tiny blades of grass had sprouted on the mound of dirt beneath which she rested. That was the way of things, he thought. In the end, nature takes back everything it has given.

"You should see the baby," he said. "He's so strong. He takes after his mother. And his eyes, as blue as the sky on a clear summer day."

There was no answer, only a warm breeze which rocked the trees in the forest beyond. He imagined the wind might carry his words to her, wherever she might be.

He stayed until dusk. When darkness had finally consumed the last ray of light, he made his way back to the house where they had made love together and talked of growing old.

The baby was asleep in a wooden cradle, snuggled among fur and animal skins. Bogdan had given him no name. Instead he waited, night after night, for Yekaterina to come in his dreams and whisper a name in his ear. But she never came, and as the weeks passed he worried he might one day forget her sweet face.

The priest, ever pious, had grown impatient and counseled him to make a decision. "It's important," the old man would say as they strolled together through the village. "He needs a name for the baptism."

Such things seemed of little consequence to him now. He'd lost his faith in God.

The house smelled of meat stew. Svyatoslav's wife stirred a large pot hung above the hearth. She'd come every day to watch the baby while he sat in silent vigil beside Yekaterina's grave.

"Supper's ready," she said.

"I'm not hungry." He was the only one in the village who'd lost weight during the winter.

"What's that got to do with anything?" She put a bowl down in front of him and forced a spoon into his hand. "Eat, or I'll bend you over my knee like I did when you were just a babe."

She was a tough woman, and he knew there was little use in arguing. He raised a spoonful to his mouth and swallowed. It tasted of garlic and onion and sent a warm sensation down his throat.

"That's better." The woman he'd known his whole life smiled. "You'll be no good to anyone, least of all the baby, if you don't eat. We can't have you wasting away."

She'd just gone back to stirring the pot when there was a knock on the door.

"That'll be my husband," she said. The pair had taken to joining him for dinner in the evenings.

The big man took a seat opposite from him at the table and helped himself to his wife's cooking. He wore a look of concern on his chiseled face. "There's some disagreement in the village."

Despite his loss, many of the villagers still sought regular guidance from Bogdan on matters big and small. His miraculous survival had not been easy for them to forget.

"Oh?"

"It's been nearly a year," said his friend, "since the eve of your sacrifice."

He took another spoonful of stew and waited for Svyatoslav to continue.

"Some say we should hold a new ceremony. They speak of old times, when many a soul vanished in the night, and argue for the safety of their children. Still others say there's no need, that the curse was broken when you survived."

They're wrong, he thought. The curse was never broken. His wife was dead, and the evil spirit still lurked in the forest. "And what of the priest? Has he anything to say?"

Svyatoslav had just finished licking his bowl clean and went back to the pot for seconds. "The priest? You know as well as anyone the priest only has eyes for miracles."

His friend was right. The priest was doing his best to spread the miracle of Bogdan the Great far and wide. There was talk of nearby villages foregoing their own ceremonies in the hopes that a single man, just a boy really, had finally put an end to the old tradition. But Bogdan had also heard the heated exchanges between the people of his village. There were those who insisted on another sacrifice, driven by fear of the spirit's revenge. A few of them had even threatened to see it through, with or without the help of the priest. It weighed on his mind in the moments when he wasn't lost in grief for his beloved wife. He tried to imagine what she might say if she was still alive to offer wise words and a steady hand. The strength he'd found in her presence diminished by the day.

"And who is next in line?"

"Young Ilya."

Ilya was a sweet boy, who had a habit of picking fresh wildflowers for his mother. Not long ago, Bogdan had been in the boy's place, though there had been no uncertainty about his fate. It must be worse, he thought, to sit idle while those who would never make such a sacrifice debate your destiny.

Svyatoslav dabbed stew from his beard. He had always been a messy eater. "The people need answers. Someone has to make a decision. I'd rather it come from you than an angry mob."

His friend was right again. He wouldn't have young Ilya dragged from the arms of his mother by villagers armed with pitchforks.

It was settled. He'd gather them together in the morning and announce his decision. He'd offer himself once more. If the spirit was determined to have his life, he could come and take it.

The old priest was unrelenting in his attempts to dissuade him. "This is madness," he said. "Do they have such little faith in the miracles of our Lord—such little faith in Bogdan the Great?"

"People don't want miracles. They know only what they can see, and deal in whispers and rumors."

"I wont—I can't allow this."

"I'm afraid it's not your decision to make."

"Then I'll have no part," said the priest. "I've spent my whole life offering up young lives to feed the evil spirit. I won't do it again."

"You must, father." He put his arm around the old man and leaned in close. "Everything must happen exactly as prescribed by tradition. Should I live, it will put an end to this once and for all. And should I die, then bury me beside my beloved."

The priest rubbed his temples. "What of the baby?"

"He will go to Svyatoslav and his honest wife, who will raise him as their own."

The old man sighed. "Are you certain I can't convince you of another course?"

Bogdan smiled. For the first time since Yekaterina's death, he felt a sense of resolve and purpose.

"I'm truly sorry," said the priest. "I'm sorry I wasn't there when it happened."

"Pay it no mind. Think only of the coming ceremony, for you shall have the honor of sending me to my death for the second time."

He sat on the same fallen tree where, one year before, he'd contemplated his fate. He was only a boy then and much had changed. He'd been married. He'd been blessed with a strong and healthy son. But still it fell on his shoulders to protect the village.

Earlier in the day, he'd said goodbye to his mother and father, brothers and sisters. Now, as the hour of the ceremony quickly approached, he wished only for peace and quiet.

There was no jubilant feast that night. No songs were sung of his glory nor was he married off to another fresh-faced wife. When the hour finally arrived, he found himself, with the priest and his closest friend by his side, leading his own procession to the edge of the forest.

Svyatoslav bound him to the tree with leather cords and kissed him on the forehead. "Go with God, my friend, and may you return to us in the morning."

The priest repeated the old legend and anointed Bogdan with holy water. The villagers prayed together, and when it was over he was left alone once again to wait for death to come.

He wasn't the only one who waited, for no sooner than they'd left did the shadowy figure emerge again from the darkness—red eyes burning in the night.

Bogdan greeted his arrival. "Here I am," he said. "Come and take my life. I am not afraid."

The evil spirit's deadly grip tightened around his throat and a heavy weight bore down upon his chest. He couldn't breath. Blood beat wildly in his ears. Everything went dark, and his final thought before the life ran out of him was of Yekaterina.

When he opened his eyes, he found himself walking in a bright field among an endless sea of wildflowers. She was there in the distance, a beautiful silhouette framed by the blue horizon—rays of sunlight shimmering in her long, blonde hair.

He called to her, the wind lifting his voice up and carrying it across the warm and open expanse. She turned and smiled. And he ran. He ran as fast as his feet could carry him.

Dawn was breaking when the cold, bony hands of the priest shook him awake. "My son," said the old man, "you still live."

A terrible pain split his head. The priest cut him down, and he stretched his stiff muscles until the blood flowed freely once more. There was the village, and the tree, and the dark forest beyond. Yekaterina was gone, and he wondered if it had only been a dream.

The villagers gathered around him as they'd done a year before, lifting him above their heads and echoing triumphant cheers. Surely, they cried, he was not only Bogdan the Great, but the greatest man to ever walk among them.

"Let there be no doubt!" The priest raised a hand and pointed to the sky. "God has heard your prayers and found cause to repeat his miracle."

At this they cheered again. But the joyous celebration was cut short by the violent screams of a woman who Bogdan recognized as young Kyrill's mother. She pushed through the crowd and threw herself at his feet. "Please, you must come."

"What's happened, good woman?"

"It's Kyrill—my handsome Kyrill." Tears streamed down the woman's face. "He's dead, Bogdan. Kyrill is dead."

ELEVEN

It was like a scene from a movie, or one of those cheap romance novels she enjoyed reading by the pool. There had always been something sexy about it, a beautiful woman staring longingly through a thick pane of plexiglass at her hot and steamy jailbird. But now, as her husband was escorted into position wearing an orange prison jumpsuit, she thought there was little to find sexy. Things were always better in books.

She lifted the plastic telephone receiver off the wall and wondered when it had last been cleaned. She tried not to think about the kind of people who might have used it before her. How silly she had been to leave the house without cleaning wipes in her purse. "What the fuck, Byron?"

"I'm sorry," he said.

"They tore up the house—even the nursery. Nora wouldn't go back to sleep for hours."

"Did they find anything?" It was obvious from the way he asked the question that it had been weighing on his mind.

She took a moment to think about how best to answer. After all, she couldn't be sure who might be listening, and thought it was stupid for her husband to ask. "Of course not. You know as well as anyone there was nothing for them to find. Still, it didn't keep them from destroying my kitchen."

He breathed a sigh of relief and rubbed his eyes with his free hand. "Please Nancy, you have to understand."

"Understand what, Byron? What am I to understand?" She was in no mood for his excuses.

"This is all just a misunderstanding. Did you speak with Mr. Bennett?"

"Briefly," she said. "He wouldn't tell me anything."

"He's busy with my case—says he'll have me back home by the end of the week."

She wasn't certain she wanted him to return home after the embarrassment he'd caused. "There were police cars in front of the house, Byron. Police cars! It's bad enough I'm stuck inside day and night with Nora, but now all of Boston will be talking."

"Let them talk."

Had he gone mad in jail? There was nothing worse than people talking, unless of course it was out of envy or admiration. "How can I ever show my face again?"

"It's just business, Nancy. These things happen. Even Martha Stewart wound up behind bars. Try to be patient. Mr. Bennett said it'll all blow over."

He was lucky there was plexiglass between them, or she would have slapped him then and there. She'd never been very good at being patient.

"I'm sorry," he said again. "I'm truly sorry." He lowered his gaze and looked back up at her with sad puppy eyes.

"Everything I did was for you and the baby. It's not so easy, you know, maintaining our lifestyle."

"Plenty of men provide far more extravagant lifestyles without winding up in jail. Daddy would never have allowed himself to be subjected to such humiliation."

"That's not fair," he said. "You know how I feel about your father."

He had good reason to be upset. Nancy's father had never approved of their marriage. Her husband was nothing more than an ambitious young upstart when they met. Even worse, he was from a working class family in the Midwest. Her father had insisted on someone from a more established family—someone who hadn't attended university on financial aid, as he'd put it. But she was full of love and big ideas. She could mold him, she'd thought all those years ago, into the man she knew he could be. An orange jumpsuit was not what she'd had in mind.

"Nancy—" He pressed a hand to the glass like a character in one of her novels. "I love you."

Perhaps it was the way he said it, or the tired and wretched look on his face, that ever so slightly softened her defenses. "Are they feeding you well?"

"Please don't ask."

She almost laughed at his sour expression. "You mean James Hook doesn't deliver in jail?" Their lobster had always been his favorite.

"Don't remind me. You'd starve to death before you ate what they feed us."

"We'll order delivery when you get home." She still wasn't sure about showing her face with him in public so soon after his unfortunate arrest.

"How's Nora?"

"She's fine. She was sleeping again when I left."

"Funny," he said. "She used to cry all the time. I thought you'd go crazy. Who's watching her?"

"Inez." It was a lie. He'd find out about the new nanny soon enough. She knew he'd be upset to learn she'd left the baby in the care of the old woman, and thought it best to avoid the discussion. He'd brought this on himself, after all, and had little say in the matter from behind bars.

A surly guard in a stiff uniform approached and put a heavy hand on her husband's shoulder. "Time's up, Hard-away."

"I love you, Nancy."

She didn't have time to respond—at least that's what she told herself—before they hurried him away.

Mr. Bennett was waiting for her in the hallway. "Nancy! How good to see you. You're looking lovely, as usual."

She'd never liked her husband's lawyer, and liked him even less for the false compliment. It was easy, she thought, to give compliments when you were billing five hundred dollars an hour. "Thank you, Anthony, though I'm afraid I didn't sleep well. I'm concerned about my husband's case."

"Don't concern yourself too much. My firm will do everything we can to see these frivolous, and might I say egregious, charges dismissed."

If there was anything she hated more than false compliments, it was to be patronized by men. She had good reason to be concerned. He was her husband. Her future, and everything she'd worked to build, was at stake. "Don't bull-shit me, Anthony. What are we talking about here?"

The lawyer's face tightened up, as if he wasn't used to being spoken to in such as way. "It's not pretty."

"I can take it," she said.

"Your husband has been charged with several felonies. It's all white collar stuff, really. Mostly just a case of bad accounting. Still, the federal government isn't taking kindly to creative bookkeeping ever since the Obama administration started cracking down on financial reporting."

"Will he go to prison?"

Mr. Bennett glanced over his shoulder. "I'm afraid this is not the appropriate place for such a discussion, but without your quick actions things could have been a lot worse. It'll be tough for them to prove intent without access to certain information. At most, he's looking at a year or two in federal prison. For now, I'm simply concerned with getting him home. There's going to be a hearing in a couple of days and the judge will set bail."

She'd never thought about what would happen if Byron went to prison. It was one of those things a busy wife blocked from her mind, as if choosing not to think about it would prevent it from coming to pass. For a quick moment, she imagined it might be nice to have the bed all to herself. At least she wouldn't have to put up with his ferocious snoring. "And best case scenario?"

The lawyer exhaled. "It all depends on the strength of the government's case. I'll have to wait for discovery to review the evidence. If you'd like to come by my office this week, we can discuss things in more detail. It's unwise to say anything further here."

"Yes," she said. "You're quite right."

"Oh, and Nancy—"

"Yes?"

"I'll have my secretary inform you of the bail hearing. It's important you attend. And bring the baby. The judge will want to see strong family ties before setting bail. Otherwise, they might consider him a flight risk."

"I can assure you," she said, "that he won't be going anywhere."

"Great." Mr. Bennett smoothed his Italian suit and straightened his silk tie. "Now if you'll excuse me, I have a meeting with the prosecutor."

"Yes, of course. Just one more question, if you don't mind my asking."

"Anything."

"Will he lose his professional license?"

"Almost certainly. Of course, the board will hold a separate hearing, but in these circumstances it's little more than a formality. Should the charges be dismissed, he can petition for reinstatement."

"Thank you, Mr. Bennett. I appreciate your candor."

She watched the man disappear down the hallway and wondered what they'd do with her husband unable to work.

The house, cursed as it was, wasn't going to pay for itself.

She was in her favorite boutique, shopping for a suitable dress for Mr. Hardaway's hearing. After a night spent tossing and turning, she'd decided not to trouble herself with money worries. Perhaps her husband's unscrupulous lawyer was right and the whole thing would simply blow over. Maybe it really had been nothing more than a few accounting errors.

"It's an excellent fit," said the young woman who managed the boutique.

Nancy agreed. She wanted to appear elegant, but not so elegant as to seem flashy. A dark, understated number by Betsy Jenney had caught her eye. It was perfect, she thought, as she stood before a vintage mirror and turned from side to side. Her figure was the only thing holding up these days.

"You look positively wonderful. May I ask, ma'am, what's the occasion?

"My husband," she said. "He's returning from a stressful business trip and I'd like to do something special."

"Oh, how thoughtful."

She'd just shimmied from the dress and passed her American Express card to the salesperson when the little bell over the door of the boutique rang. Two women entered arm in arm. Nancy recognized them as the Sybill sisters—perfectly styled from head to toe in the season's latest fashion. It was easy for them, she thought. Their husbands had both come from wealthy families and died, rather conveniently, in the same small plane crash during a shared holiday on the Maine coast. The sisters had hardly pretended to mourn. Just weeks after their husbands were buried, they'd returned to hosting some of the most extravagant social affairs in Boston. Nancy was always invited, though it had been months since she'd last been in attendance.

"Nancy!" It was Karen Sybill, the younger and rounder of the two, who spoke first. "We haven't seen you in ages. I do hope you're holding up in light of recent events."

She recognized it for what it was—an insult rather than a sincere expression of good wishes. Word must have spread quickly of her husband's arrest. She knew better than to let them see her discomfort, and worked to maintain a smile.

The older sister spoke next. "How's the baby, dear?"

"Nora? Oh, she's fine."

"Have you managed to find a replacement nanny?"

It was another veiled insult. "Why yes, in fact the nanny is watching Nora while I do my shopping."

A surprised look crossed the woman's face. "So glad to hear it, Nancy. Is she French? No, I'm aware of only two French nannies and they're already engaged. Perhaps she's Mexican?"

"Canadian, actually."

"French Canadian?"

It seemed like a pointless question, though one she would have asked not long ago. "Ukrainian. But she was born and raised in Newfoundland."

"How fascinating. Ukraine? Isn't that somewhere in Europe?"

Nancy had decided she was tired of their questions, and was relieved when the salesperson motioned her over to the counter.

"I'm very sorry, ma'am, but there seems to be a problem with your card."

"Try it again, please."

"I've tried it twice already. It could be our card reader. Sometimes these things happen. Maybe you'd like to try a different card?"

"Yes, of course." She passed the young woman her Visa card and did her best to appear unbothered.

The sisters, always on high alert for any deviancy from good social standards, had noticed her exchange with the salesperson and were zeroing in their attention like cats stalking prey.

"I'm sorry," said the young woman. "The Visa card's not working either. Can I offer you the use of our phone to call your bank? I'm sure it's just a misunderstanding."

She'd been a regular at the boutique for years, and not once had her cards been declined. They should give it to her on credit, she thought, or least do a better job of not making a scene. The Sybill sisters would tell everyone she'd gone broke. "That's quite alright," she said. "I'll pick it up tomorrow."

"Is there a problem, Nancy?" Karen's round face stared back at her.

"It's the alterations. They won't be finished until tomorrow." It was her best attempt at a diversion. But it was hopeless. Karen was already smiling.

"There's no reason to be ashamed. I'll swipe my card and you can pay me back later. I'm quite certain you're good for the money. Better yet, consider it a gift."

She would have rather died right there, spread out on the marble floor with blood pooling beneath her like the poor nanny, before accepting charity from the likes of the Sybill sisters. It was too late to save face. Half the people in Boston, at least the half that mattered, would soon be talking about her.

She clutched her purse and ran from the boutique. Her head spun as she struggled for breath on the sidewalk. It was an all-too-familiar feeling, the onset of a panic attack. The psychiatrist had a fancy name for it, but the only thing that mattered now was the little blue pill she took from a small plastic container and swallowed.

TWELVE

The scent of a thousand wildflowers filled the air. The sun warmed his skin. It was a place he'd been before, even if it was only a dream. Was he dreaming again? He didn't know and didn't care. Who could say what was real and what was a dream?

The only thing that mattered was her—more beautiful than ever—wearing the same white dress he'd lifted gently over her shoulders on the night of their wedding.

"Hello," she said, "I'm here."

He tried to speak, but when he opened his mouth the words wouldn't form on his lips.

She took him by the hand—a delicate touch—and they ran through green fields until they fell together to the earth and made love. It was as it had always been, not just two bodies, but two timeless souls joined together in one eternal moment. Not even her death could destroy it.

"Bogdan—" The soft touch of her fingers upon his cheek sent a pleasant shiver down his spine. "—you must go now, my love."

He didn't want to go. He wanted to stay lost with her in the dream from which he knew he would soon wake.

"You must go. The people need you."

The people always needed him. He was born to die for them, and had given up everything, including the one he loved. Let me dream a little longer, he thought. Was it too much to ask?

But someone else was calling his name now. "Bogdan. Wake up, Bogdan."

"Don't go," he said to her. "Please don't go."

She smiled one last time and fell away like the leaves fall from the trees in autumn. He clung to her, but there was nothing in the place where she had been.

"Bogdan, you must come." Svyatoslav stood above him in the dark space of the room. The big man shook him with a rough hand until he stirred and rubbed the sleep from his eyes. A heavy rain battered the roof and ran in wet streaks down the glass of the window.

"What's happened?"

His friend fed a log into the hearth, and the room was lit by the faint glow of crackling sparks. "It's Oleksander."

"What of him?"

"He's dead, Bogdan. His wife woke to find him cold and lifeless in the bed beside her."

Bogdan rubbed his tired eyes and struggled against the pull of his warm bed. It had been less than a week since they buried young Kyrill in a grave not far from where Yekaterina rested. He'd slept little in the days and nights that followed. "Did you fetch the priest?"

"Yes." Svyatoslav poked at the embers of the fire, sending sparks swirling up into the darkness. "I'm sorry, Bogdan. He told me to bring you."

The priest would never let him rest. A man's death was the concern of the church. Oleksander, though not particularly old, was old enough to have died in his sleep the way most men pass when their time has come. He wondered why the priest would have need of him at such an early hour. If only he could sleep again, perhaps Yekaterina would return. But he knew there was little chance. His thoughts had already been stirred and sleep wouldn't come.

They made their way across the muddy clearing to the house where Oleksander lived with his family. Bogdan's cloak was wet and his boots tracked mud across the threshold as they ducked inside. But Oleksander's wife paid it little mind. She was crying in a corner, blankets wrapped around her tiny frame, while a woman Bogdan recognized as her sister worked to console her.

The priest stood beside the bed in his long, black robes, reciting a prayer for the dead in a language Bogdan didn't understand. The old man stopped to acknowledge his arrival only when he'd finished making the sign of the cross in the air above Oleksander's lifeless body. "Bogdan the Great," he said. "I'm quite relieved to see you here. I wouldn't trouble you at such an hour unless I had cause for concern."

"What is it, priest?"

The old man took his wrist with a bony hand and pulled him into the far corner of the house. "This is the work of the Devil."

Bogdan couldn't be sure what he meant. Perhaps the old man had also been suffering from sleepless nights since Kyrill's early death. "Are you well, father?"

The priest tightened his grip on Bogdan's wrist. "You must listen, Bogdan. I beg of you, please listen to Oleksander's wife."

He had no desire to listen to anyone, but he would do as the priest asked. Svyatoslav wrapped the body in linens, and when the wife had regained some small sense of composure, they gathered together around the table in the kitchen.

She sniveled and worked to hold back her tears as she muttered something about a strange visitor. "He comes in the night."

"Who comes?"

Her eyes widened like the eyes of a deer the moment a hunter's arrow found flesh. "I'm afraid, my lord."

"I'm not your lord, good woman. But I wish to know what's been troubling you."

"It's a dark figure," she said. "There's a crushing weight upon my chest. I can't move. I can't breath. And the eyes, oh Dear Lord, the eyes—red as hot coals in the fire." She burst into tears again, her body shaking and rocking side to side beneath the blankets.

The priest reached across the table and took her trembling hands in his own, the same way he'd taken Bogdan's hands after Yekaterina's death. "Rest now, for your husband is joined with the angels in the Kingdom of Heaven."

The poor widow's sister, joined by Svyatoslav's wife with her herbs and salves, consoled her as the men stepped out into the rain. Svyatoslav lit his pipe and they passed it around. In the distance, the first sliver of light fought against the dark storm clouds towering overhead.

"Could it be?" The priest still spoke in a hushed tone.

Spring was supposed to be a time of life, a time of blooming flowers and full plates and work to be done in the fields. But for Bogdan and the people of the village, spring had brought the sickly smell of death. If the woman had indeed seen a pair of red eyes glowing through the dark, it could only mean he wasn't alone in being haunted by the evil spirit. "Tell me, priest, what of your miracles now?"

The old man raised the hood of his cloak to shield himself from the rain. "Who could say why God allows such beasts to roam the earth?"

Svyatoslav drew a long, deep breath through his pipe and exhaled a thick line of smoke. "What does he want?"

Bogdan took the pipe and drew his own deep breath. He knew then his own survival had left the spirit in need of the very thing which sustained it. "He's hungry, and he wants revenge."

THIRTEEN

She'd had to settle for an old dress, a cheap, off-the-rack number she'd last worn years ago to the funeral of her husband's aunt. It was a tired shade of black and made her shoulders look uneven, but the lawyer had told her not to wear anything flashy. Besides, she couldn't risk her credit cards being declined at another boutique. In the days since Byron's arrest, she'd gone so far as to withdraw cash from her personal savings account, and was going around with a stack of bills in her purse like the wife of a drug lord.

He'd come by the house earlier, the lawyer, to pick up a suit for Mr. Hardaway to wear in court. She'd suggested a single-button ensemble her husband had custom tailored during a ski trip to Northern Italy, but the lawyer selected another cheap, off-the-rack special.

"It's best not to appear rich," he'd said.

"And what about the credit cards?" She was eager to resume her normal spending habits.

"There's a bank freeze. It's only temporary. Hold tight until things settle down."

Nancy didn't want to hold tight—whatever that meant. The ladies were already talking, and the only way to set them straight would be a public display of spending. If only she could walk into some well-trafficked boutique and make a large purchase, or better yet, give a substantial donation to a fashionable charity, at least the rumors about any financial difficulties would be silenced.

As for her husband's arrest, she hoped with enough time they'd grow bored of speaking about it. She knew no better way to make a comeback than to be seen wining and dining around town.

She was strangely optimistic as she put the final touches on her makeup. The hearing would take place in one hour, and she imagined it was possible the whole matter might be settled. Mr. Bennett, despite whatever distaste she had for him, really was one of the finest lawyers in Boston, and he'd gone to great lengths to convince her it was all just a huge misunderstanding.

Inez, ready as always, was waiting in her usual position at the bottom of the stairs. "The driver called," she said. "He should be here any moment. Don't worry about Nora. I'll keep an eye on things while you're away."

They were joined by the old Ukrainian. "No need. Baby Nora is quite safe in my care."

Inez flashed the nanny a suspicious glance. They'd been on cordial terms since Iryna had moved in with nothing more than her small bag, but the growing distance between them had not gone unnoticed by Nancy. Indeed, they'd hardly said a word to each other beyond the expected formalities.

Nancy had more pressing things to concern herself with than the staff playing nice. Should all go well at the court-

house, she'd be returning with her husband in tow. She'd
kept her decision to employ the nanny a secret and would
accept no protest from her husband. It was he who owed her
an explanation, she'd decided, not the other way around.

Either way, she'd held up her end of the bargain and per-
formed well under pressure. A smile formed on her tight lips
as she recalled the rush of feeding her husband's documents
into the shredder—the only solid evidence of any wrongdo-
ing. Her father had been wrong all those years, she could
handle herself when the going got tough.

Mr. Bennett greeted her at the courthouse—he was all
smiles and reassurances as he ushered her into one of the
courtrooms. He helped her to a row of long benches before
taking his own seat at a desk in the front of the room.

She was relieved to see her husband wearing the boring
suit the lawyer had retrieved as a pair of officers escorted him
into position beside Mr. Bennett. She'd decided after her
first visit to jail that the orange jumpsuit was not a flattering
look. Those romance novels, she thought, had been full of
shit. Her husband smiled and gave a tiny nod in her direction as he passed. It was his way of telling her not worry,
that everything would be okay.

The officers called the room to order and an old judge
appeared from a side door. He was dressed in the customary
black robe and wore a stern look on his face. Nancy felt a
pang of doubt when she caught site of the old man's expression. He hardly seemed one for easy resolutions.

Whatever resolutions she'd hoped for hadn't come. It
was as the high-priced lawyer had said, just a preliminary

hearing. The charges were even more serious than she'd imagined. Felony tax evasion. Felony embezzlement. Felony bank fraud. Her husband pleaded not guilty and the grizzled old judge set bail at $500,000. With a quick bang of the gavel, it was over as quickly as it had begun.

"Nancy? Nancy Hardaway?"

She turned toward whoever had called her name, and saw a somewhat younger woman whose face she vaguely recognized. "Yes," she said. "Can I help you?"

"Do you remember me?"

She tried to recall the woman's name and drew a blank. Perhaps she'd been at one of the many charity events she'd attended over the years. "I'm sorry, dear. I've been rather preoccupied lately. Was it the war veteran's fundraiser?"

The younger woman's face twisted up as though she was holding back frustration. "No, it wasn't the veteran's fundraiser. Maybe you remember my husband, Carter Reynolds?"

"Oh, yes! How could I forget Carter?" She had no idea who the woman was talking about. "How is he?"

"He's dead."

"Oh, I'm terribly sorry to hear that." There was something about the woman that said this was more than just a friendly chat, a moment of spontaneous recognition in an otherwise faceless crowd. Nancy started toward the door, where her husband's lawyer already waited. "Excuse me, dear. I hate to be rude, but I don't have time to catch up."

"Aren't you just the least bit curious?" The woman's voice was bitter. Hostile. "Aren't you curious about how he died?"

"No, that's a personal matter and I wouldn't dare intrude. Now if you'll please excuse me—the lawyer is quite costly and he doesn't like to be kept waiting."

The younger woman scoffed. "Oh, please. It's not like you don't have the money. You and your husband have been stealing from people for a long time."

Who was this woman to accuse her of such things? She wasn't about to wait around to find out. Mr. Bennett stepped out into the marble-lined hallway and Nancy joined him. The woman followed close on her heels and didn't seem likely to give up.

The lawyer, for his part, sensed the tension between them and tried his best to intervene on Nancy's behalf. "I'm Anthony Bennett," he said, as he held out a hand. "I don't think we've had the pleasure of meeting."

"Save it," said the young Mrs. Reynolds. "You should know you're defending a murderer."

Nancy couldn't stomach it any longer. Byron might be a cheater and a liar, but she could be sure he'd never killed anyone. Besides, he was never the type to get his hands dirty. "How dare you?" The blood rose up from her chest and choked the words in her throat. She took a moment to compose herself before continuing. "Look, I'm sorry about whatever happened to your husband, but I think you might be confused. I was only being polite. I've never seen you before in all my life."

It was a lie. Now that she'd had a good look at the angry young woman, she remembered her from a debutante ball at one of the hotels near the Theater District. It was a rather tired affair, but Byron had pressed her to come along. One of his many business partners, a heavyset man with a funny name she couldn't recall, had an equally plump daughter who was making her debut to Boston society.

"Don't play games, Nancy. You were quite friendly the night we met. You even insisted on introducing my poor

Carter to your scoundrel husband. He was always one to trust too easily, my sweet man." The woman's eyes filled with shiny tears. "He invested our life savings into one of your husband's can't-fail opportunities—even took out a second mortgage on the house."

Mr. Bennett, with his expensive Italian suit and designer briefcase, positioned himself between the two of them and took Nancy by the arm. "Please," he said. "This really isn't the place."

Nancy didn't like where the conservation was going and made no protest as he led her toward the exit.

But the woman was relentless in her pursuit. Her voice rose above the crowd milling about in the busy hallway. "We lost everything to your husband's scam. Everything."

They'd almost made it to the car when the woman caught up with them in the parking lot.

"He killed himself, Nancy."

They climbed into the backseat of the hired sedan and locked the door. The woman pounded on the side of the car, screaming and running beside them as the driver backed out and pulled away.

"He's dead," she wailed. "He's dead!"

Inez, sensing her discomfort, had been thoughtful enough to draw a hot bath and light her favorite scented candles. Not even the familiar scent of lavender could clear the image of the young woman from her head. She closed her eyes and sunk deeper into the water, as if she might wash the whole thing away. But all she could see was the woman running beside the car, crying out in anger and despair.

People lose money all the time, she told herself. It was part of the game. Those without the stomach for it shouldn't play. How could she or her husband be responsible for someone else's bad luck? Byron would be home soon. He'd explain everything and clear up this awful mess.

She'd almost found some comfort in the thought when she heard a commotion outside the house. She slipped a robe over her shoulders and peered through the bathroom window, half expecting to see more government agents gathering for another raid. What she saw was even worse.

Just outside the front door, on the street she'd called home for the last eight years, a line of news vans and their respective camera crews assembled.

FOURTEEN

Panic spread like wildfire through the village. Anxious mothers stayed awake at night to stand watch over their children, rousting them at even the smallest sign of a bad dream. They were exhausted, with little time to tend the fields. Life had all but come to a complete stop in their tiny corner of the world.

Bogdan's back ached, but he made no complaints. Svyatoslav worked beside him, their shovels alternating in somber rhythm. It was the seventh grave they'd dug in as many weeks.

The morning had begun like so many others, with the shrill scream of a mother or wife waking to find a child or husband dead. That particular morning, it had been Volodymyr, the village's faithful blacksmith, who was found, drained of life, by the woman who'd been his wife for thirty-two years.

The priest, though reluctant to abandon them, had left some days before for a nearby village. "We should know," he'd said, "if it's happening to the others."

His absence meant there would be no one to say the final prayer over Volodymyr's grave, but the funeral would have to continue without him. Summer had arrived, and it was too hot to leave the body until he returned. Death lingered over everything, and they were reminded well enough without the smell of a rotting corpse.

When the hole had been dug, they wiped the dirt from their brows and sipped water from wooden cups. Svyatoslav was the first to speak. "It should be you who leads the prayers for the departed. The people are tired, yet still they look to you for strength in these darkest of days."

Bogdan shrugged. His most loyal of friends was only being generous. The village was small, and he'd heard rumors of the people's whisperings. "They blame me."

Svyatoslav took another sip and poured cool water over his dirt-stained face. "They're weak, Bogdan. And afraid. They want answers."

The big man always spoke the truth. It was the rarest of traits among men.

"Who am I to give the answers they seek? A year ago, I was just a boy." He motioned to the nearby tree where he'd been bound and left to die.

"A boy who lived."

Yes, he thought. They never hesitated to remind him. But as the days and months dragged on, his miraculous survival had revealed itself for what it really was—a terrible curse. "If only she was still here," he said, "she'd know what to do."

"She was always stronger than you." Svyatoslav's eyes fell upon the place where Yekaterina rested. Fresh grass covered the dirt above her grave. "What would become of men without the strength of women?"

It was the women who suffered the most, he thought. If it wasn't the evil spirit's insatiable thirst which took their men and children, it would be hunger, disease, and war.

His friend held out a calloused hand. "Come and rest now. We've done enough digging for one day."

But he was too angry for rest. How could he, Bogdan the Great, rest his bones while those around him died? No, he thought, a chair had served little use while Yekaterina bled dry on the bed beside him. He raised the shovel high in the air and took another stab at the earth.

Svyatoslav shrugged his shoulders and fell back into place beside him, the alternating rhythm of their shovels marking a burial hymn for one who had not yet come to pass. "How many more will we dig?"

"I don't know," he said. "How many more souls remain in our village?"

They were vigilant now. Torches were lit, their dancing flames ringed the village and cast bouncing shadows upon the trees at the edge of the forest. Outside every door, an able-bodied man stood guard, or in the absence of a man, one of the older boys—tired and frightened looks on their slender faces. Svyatoslav went among them with his pipe, slapping them across their slumping backs and feeding them smoke to keep them awake. Inside, the women gathered and drank tea and hovered nervously over sleeping babes. This night, they had resolved themselves, would not claim the life of another.

Bogdan strode back and forth before a large bonfire at the center of the village. The priest, who'd only just returned from his journey to the neighboring settlements, followed closely at his side. Black robes swished and spun in the orange glow of the fire as the older man struggled to keep pace.

"Tell me," said Bogdan, "what has become of the others? Have they, too, fallen victim to that most evil curse which comes in the night?"

The priest stroked his beard. It had become a familiar sight to Bogdan, and could only mean something weighed heavily on the pious man's mind. "Yes," said the priest. "Some of them have, but not all."

"Only some?"

"The people mustn't know, Bogdan." He gathered his black robes and held them tightly around his chest. "There are some things in life, some secrets, which they are not meant to understand."

He struggled to make sense of what the old priest had said. People were dying. It was not the time for keeping secrets. "And what of me? Am I not meant to understand?"

"You, my dearest boy, are the only one who can."

He stopped pacing and lifted his eyes to meet the old man's weary gaze. He said nothing, choosing to wait in silence as if it might urge the priest's words to fill the empty space between them.

It was some time before the priest finally spoke. "You've buried many fine men these days."

"Some men," he said. "Some boys."

"I'm sorry, my son. Do you remember the story of Jesus?"

"How could I forget? I lost many a fine summer afternoon of playing in the woods while you recited endlessly the story of our Lord and Savior."

"Then I've served you well, Bogdan the Great." The old man's tired face shifted into the weakest of smiles, which vanished as quickly as it had appeared. "And what of the other story—that of the beast who was once only a man, and who haunts us now in our sleep?"

"Yes, priest. I remember." He'd spent his whole life beneath the shadow of that story. And while he'd been spared from his own early end, it was only to watch those around him fall one after another. He'd passed many a late hour wondering if it would have been better to die a simple death, as so many others had done before him.

"Good," said the old man. "For hundreds of years, the men of my faith have sent young boys to die a martyr's death. But unlike our Lord Jesus, there is no resurrection, no triumphant return. We loathe it. It goes against all that we believe, you see, to satisfy the desires of the Devil. Yet like men so often do, we went along with such wickedness, if only so that others might have lived."

The priest placed a hand on Bogdan's shoulders. Despite the summer heat and the roar of the nearby bonfire, his fingers were cold and stiff. Bogdan longed for Yekaterina's soft touch.

"It was a task passed from one generation to another, men of the cloth working in secret. The Church, for all its worldly knowledge and wisdom, turned a blind eye. It was a local matter, they declared in closed meetings behind heavy doors. But then one fateful day, there was a boy who gave himself up to death and returned, as our Lord and Savior returned."

"Me?"

"Yes, my son."

"I'm no savior, father."

"No, my son. There can be only one Savior, and his name is Jesus Christ. But you became something else—something the people prayed for each night as they put themselves down for bed. My dear sweet Bogdan, you gave them, for the first time in more than a century, that most important thing—hope."

Perhaps he was wrong, Bogdan thought. Maybe hope was nothing more than a fool's errand, or worse, something which invited danger in like a kind-hearted family giving shelter to a murderous stranger. "But what of the other villages?"

"Have you not listened, boy? When word spread of your return, there were some, much the same as ourselves, who took joy in your victory and found solace in the Devil's defeat. They were no less tired of sacrificing their children than we. It was a custom long overdue for a swift end."

"They stopped making the sacrifice?"

The priest nodded. "Yes, Bogdan the Great. When they learned of your triumph they cast off the old traditions and sent their children to die no longer."

"Now they pay the price." It was bad enough to imagine himself as the cause of his own village's suffering, but they were not alone. Others suffered as well, and he was to blame. "And what of those who continued the sacrifice?"

"Ah," said the old man. His bony hand, still resting upon Bogdan's shoulder, grew heavy as if he might buckle beneath some great invisible burden. "Their sacrifices were sent to an early grave, but the rest of the villagers have been spared."

So it was true. The evil spirit had only come to claim his bitter revenge on those who had dared to defy him. "Then the ceremony must resume."

"It cannot," said the priest. His eyes reflected the swirling flames of the bonfire. "The others will not be told—this must remain a secret."

"But why?" It had never been in the old man's nature to keep secrets, and Bogdan failed to understand the reason for his deception. "Lives can be saved."

The priest sighed. "You may be right, but how many more years can this continue? Fifty? A hundred? A thousand? How many mothers and fathers must give their young to feed a curse that's plagued our lands for as long as anyone can remember?"

"What would you have us do?"

The old man dropped his grip from Bogdan's shoulder and lowered his eyes to the ground. "I don't know. But I choose to believe—no, I must believe—that a boy who survived the beast not only once, but twice, holds the key to ridding ourselves of this evil once and for all."

Though nothing the priest had said was funny, Bogdan couldn't help but laugh. It was the desperate laugh of a man who had no other choice than to find humor in such impossible circumstances.

"Do you think me a fool?"

It was his turn to take the old man by the shoulder. "Look around. Yekaterina is dead. Kyrill is dead. How can I possibly be the one to end this curse?"

A spark returned to the priest's eyes. "You were always such a sad and lonesome boy. The other children would call out your name and you'd pretend not to hear them, preferring instead to wander alone into the forest and spend hours lost in thought. Yekaterina, may God rest her soul, was the only one who could draw you back. But there was one thing you enjoyed more than being alone."

Bogdan smiled as he remembered the stories the old man used to tell as they'd gather around a late night fire. They were from the Bible, and though Bogdan had never taken much interest in religion, the priest had a way of bringing the stories to life in a way no dusty old book ever could. Bogdan would sit crosslegged at his mother's feet, vivid images racing through his mind, as the priest spoke of strange men in foreign lands who did the work of a God who was both cruel and forgiving. "How could I ever forget the stories you'd tell?"

The priest smiled back at him. "Then surely you remember the Book of Job?"

"Job?" While he'd always enjoyed the old man's skillful story-telling, the specifics had been lost to the passage of time.

"Yes, dear Bogdan. As a man of faith, I should love all of God's revelations with equal fervor, though I must admit the Book of Job has always been my favorite."

"Tell me again." It would be a useful distraction to hear the priest recite one of his many stories.

"Well—" The old man cleared his throat. "I'm afraid there isn't time for the finer details, but it goes something like this: There lived in Uz a man named Job, who was known across the land for his faith and prosperity. All those with whom he conducted business were blessed with good fortune, until one day his luck changed. You see, God, in all his wisdom, granted the Devil permission to tempt Job away from his Divine Grace. Soon Job's fortune was diminished, and he found himself in grave poverty. His daughters fell ill and died. And his friends—full of feverish restlessness and false counsel—cursed whatever wrath God had certainly set upon him."

"Ah, yes," said Bogdan. "But Job, despondent as though he was, would not bring himself to curse God's name. He accepted his suffering as the will of the Lord."

"I shall die a happy man, my son. For the toils of a sad old priest have not been entirely lost on the children of my flock. But I wonder, do you remember what happens to that most faithful of men in the end?"

"He was restored to even greater prosperity than before, and blessed with seven more daughters—the most beautiful in the land."

"Yes, said the priest. "And so, like Job, we must remain patient in our suffering. This curse will not last forever. There will come a day in the future when men and women will speak of a horror long past as though it was only a fable, and their children will abound with joyful innocence. You ask what we must do, my son. I cannot say, but the Lord will lead us back into the light if only we might accept his divine will."

They were strong and compelling words, uttered with the conviction of a man of unshakeable faith. "Very well," he said. "I will keep your secret, priest—at least for now."

"Thank you." The old man kissed him on the forehead and charged into the night, black robes swishing in the dying light of the bonfire before he was swallowed whole by the darkness.

The curtains did little to block the early morning daylight pouring in through the window. He slept in fitful bouts, his dreams afflicted by the many horrors set upon in them in the previous weeks.

The priest's words had sent his thoughts spinning. If it was true—if the villages who'd continued the ceremony had lost only one of their own and no more, then the spirit had not unleashed his wrathful vengeance upon them. But what of the others—what could be done to lift the curse and break the cycle of suffering?

He'd just drifted back into something resembling a nightmare when a mother's wail arose from a nearby house. This time, it wasn't enough to startle him. He'd grown accustomed to the sorry sounds and was almost surprised on the mornings when no one was found dead.

Their vigilance had been in vain. The torches had done little to fend off the intruder. We've lost another, he thought, as he pulled on his boots and steadied himself for the tears and anguish that would greet him.

FIFTEEN

She watched from the bedroom window—camera crews encircling a black sedan as it slowed to a stop in front of the house. Mr. Bennett was the first to exit. His attempt to wave the reporters off was almost comical, a small man in a designer suit flapping his arms around like some kind of bird. They only pressed in closer, like ravenous vultures crowding around a dead carcass, to greet her husband as he stepped out of the vehicle.

Worse yet, the neighbors were watching the spectacle unfold from across the street. Sure, embezzlement, bank fraud, and tax evasion were crimes in their own right. But among the high society families, there was no greater crime than drawing unwanted attention to their doorsteps.

How she hated her husband now for the shame he'd caused their family. It was a good thing her father was dead, because she never would have heard the end of it. She imagined him in one of his ridiculous golf outfits, whiskey sour in one hand and a cigar in the other, as the old man prattled on about the other men she could have married.

As the spectacle unfolded on the street below, another image crept into her head. It was the face of the young woman from the courthouse, tears rolling down her cheeks as she described her husband losing their savings, and eventually, taking his own life. These things happen, she told herself. People lose money all the time. Surely, Byron wasn't solely to blame. Still, the woman's sobs had haunted her since that day.

Her thoughts were interrupted by the sound of the front door swinging shut. She found some relief in the sight of the reporters and camera crews returning to their vans. Byron would no doubt be waiting for her in the study.

"I'm sorry, Nancy," was all he managed to say before turning his attention to the disheveled drawers of the desk and filing cabinet. Inez had attempted to return some order to the room after the police raid, but Nancy insisted she leave the task to her husband. "Are you certain they didn't find anything?"

"I did exactly what you told me to do, Byron." Was it too much, she thought, to expect a more sophisticated apology? He could have at least stopped along the way to buy fresh flowers.

"What did they take?"

"A few boxes of paperwork from the desk drawers."

"And the shredder?" He was still rummaging through whatever they'd left behind. "Where's the shredder?"

"Oh, they took that, too."

"Jesus Christ, Nancy. Did you at least empty it first?"

"I didn't have time." She couldn't guess what the problem was. "It's not like you gave me a lot of notice. Just imagine what would have happened if I had been out with the ladies."

"Great," he said. "That's just great. You know they can put all those little pieces of paper back together again. They have people who do that."

"What?" She almost felt sorry for whoever's job it might be to sort through all those tiny shreds and put them back together. "I had no idea."

"Maybe if you weren't so busy worrying about what all those fussy ladies think, you'd have time to consider these things." He ran his fingers through his hair as his eyes darted around the room. "If they trace those account numbers, I'm sunk."

"You have some nerve, Byron Hardaway, blaming me for this like it's my doing. Is it true what the papers say? Did you really steal from all those people—from the people we call our friends?"

"Oh, come on," he said. "Don't pretend like you're innocent, Nancy. You had no problem spending the money. Those fancy designer dresses—a house like this—these things don't just pay for themselves."

She wanted to slap him across the face. "You never told me it was stolen."

For a moment, he looked as though he might jump across the desk and strangle her. Nancy watched as he took a deep breath and composed himself, poured a drink and offered her one.

She declined.

"Look," he said. "I didn't steal anything. It's not like I put a gun to anyone's head. It's all in the accounting."

"Are you going to prison?" It was the question she'd wanted to ask since the day of his arrest. Sure, she'd asked the lawyer, but getting a straight answer from that man was next to impossible.

He took a sip of cognac. "Do you want the truth or do you want me to make you feel better?"

"Tell me," she said. "I need to know."

"It's possible. It's a complicated situation—things could go either way."

At least he wasn't holding that back from her. She took a seat on the leather sofa and smoothed her dress. "What about the credit cards? Mr. Bennett said something about a bank hold."

"They froze our assets pending investigation. I was hoping the cards in your name would still work."

"I didn't even know they could do that. How are we going to pay for things? There's the matter of Inez's salary, never mind the caretaker and the nanny." She tried to catch the last word as it slipped off her tongue.

Too late.

"What nanny? I thought we'd stopped looking."

"The old woman," she said. "I needed help with Nora while you were away."

"But, Nancy—"

"What, Byron? I won't argue this with you."

"We can hardly afford to pay Inez. If it wasn't for the money I secured in Nora's trust, we might lose the house."

"You're a clever man. I'm sure you can find some way to make it work."

"Besides," he said, "I don't like that woman. Something about her isn't quite right. The way she just showed up at our door like that in the dead of night—it gives me the creeps."

As if on cue, the old woman appeared in the doorway. "I'm sorry to disturb you. I only wanted to welcome Mr. Hardaway back home. I do hope they were kind."

Nancy wondered if she'd heard what her husband had said about her. "Iryna, please come and have a drink. We were just saying how nice it is to have your help with Nora. She's really taken a liking to you."

"Oh, it's my pleasure. She's really such an angel. You should be very proud."

"We are," said Mr. Hardaway. "Now if you'll please excuse us, we have important matters to discuss."

The old woman smiled. "Can I bring you anything? Nora's down for her afternoon nap and I'm afraid I'm not much use to anyone wandering alone around the house. Perhaps you'd like something to eat with your cognac? You really shouldn't drink on an empty stomach. They say it's quite unhealthy."

Nancy had spent enough time around the women of Boston to recognize the insult hidden behind such an innocent question. Byron could fuss until he was blue in the face. She was starting to like the old woman more each day.

"No, thanks," said her husband. "I'm sure Inez will prepare a wonderful dinner."

Iryna bobbed her head as she ducked from the room and disappeared back into the empty space of the big house. She's light on her feet, thought Nancy, for such an old woman. It had given her great pleasure to watch Iryna take a stab at Byron.

"As I was saying, Nancy."

"You're always saying something."

"We don't have the money, at least not while the bulk of our assets are frozen. You can keep the nanny if you like, but the caretaker will have to go."

"He has a son," she said. The boy was seven or eight, the product of a previous marriage, and lived with his laconic father in the basement apartment. Nancy had hoped he might play with Nora when she was old enough.

"I'm sorry, but we can't afford three salaries, and we're not getting rid of Inez. Nobody cooks like that woman." He rubbed his belly as though he might eat something after all. "You said you want to make decisions, Nancy, so make a decision. Will it be the caretaker or the nanny?"

The slender man's head hung low and heavy. She'd found him trimming the hedges in their small garden while his son rode a bicycle in circles on the back patio.

"I'm sorry, Leroy."

"Don't be sorry, Mrs. Hardaway. You're not the only one who's ever fallen on bad times. These things happen. I understand."

Bad times? He pities me, she thought. It was the first time she'd ever been pitied by someone as low in life as a simple caretaker. Were things really that bad? "We'll pay you through the end of the month, of course."

"If it's not too much trouble, do you think my son and I could stay on in the apartment? I could still help out around the property, you know, in place of rent. The boy is just so happy in school and I'd hate to move him to another district."

It felt good to consider his request. It meant she was no longer being pitied. Instead, she was in a position to grant favors. Besides, it was nice having someone around to look after the place. The hedges weren't going to trim themselves. "I'll have to discuss it with Mr. Hardaway, but I don't see any reason why that would be a problem."

"Thank you, Mrs. Hardaway. That's very kind. I always knew you were good people. I can't fathom all the things they're saying about your husband are true."

"Yes, well—there's no need for thanks. It's the least we could do after so many years of loyal service."

The whole exchange had gone rather well. It was the first time she'd fired anyone, and it hadn't been nearly as dreadful as she'd imagined—though she would have preferred he kept the comments about her husband to himself. She didn't like being reminded. It was bad enough with all the reporters drawn to the house like sharks to blood in the water. Poor Inez had no choice but to slip out through the back gate and scramble down the alley on her way back home that evening. Nancy wondered how long all the negative attention might possibly last.

Still, she was feeling especially good about her charitable act of kindness. Byron, lost among the stacks of paperwork in his study, hadn't even put up a fight when she announced the caretaker would continue occupying what would otherwise be an empty apartment.

It was well after dark when the last of the news crews retreated for the night. Finally at liberty to relax, she'd just drawn herself a hot bath when she was startled by a loud slap against the glass of the bedroom window. It was followed seconds later by another slap.

Then another.

"Byron!" She switched off the lights and crept toward the window, but she couldn't make out anything in the darkness beyond. "Please, come quick!"

She heard her husband fumble as he rushed up the stairs. He was short of breath and red in the face when he joined her at the window. "What is it? What did you see?"

"There was a strange noise, like someone might be trying to break in."

Just then there was another loud slap against the window, followed by something slimy sliding down the glass.

On the street below, a group of teenage boys had gathered and were passing around cartons of fresh eggs.

"It's just kids," said her husband. He opened the window just in time to get hit squarely in the face with an egg. "Get lost, punks! I'm calling the police!"

Nancy couldn't help but laugh.

SIXTEEN

It wasn't Bogdan who betrayed the priest, but a traveling merchant on his way through the village.

"That's an awful lot of graves," he said, as he peddled his wares to a somber crowd. "You're not the only ones."

"Yes," said one of the men. "It's happening all over the countryside."

"Not exactly," said the merchant. "Some of the villages have been spared."

They pushed in close around him and demanded to know more. "Tell us," they said. "Who has been spared?"

By the time Bogdan caught word of what was happening it was too late. The crowd had transformed into an angry mob. There was nothing he could do to stop them as they gathered on the steps of the wooden church, pounding on the door with clenched fists.

"Priest!" Some of the men waved pitchforks and sickles in the air. "Why have you not told us of the others—that those who continued the ceremony have escaped the terrible fate which has befallen us?"

The priest tried to calm them. "Please, my children. You must understand. Whatever trespass I've committed against you was for good reason."

Bogdan thought they might kill him. He should say something, he thought from his place at the back of the crowd. But what was there to say? It was only when one of the men stepped forward and took the horrified priest by his neck that Bogdan emerged and stood before them.

"You are my friends," he said. "You are my family. Please, listen to what the priest has to say. He has loved many of us since we were only children, and would never conspire with an agent of the Devil against us."

"You knew?" It was the wife of one of the men who'd spoken first. "We trusted you. We believed in you."

"I never asked you to believe in me. I was only a boy sent to die, who somehow lived."

"Let's not forget," said the priest, who'd managed to free himself from the man's grip. "Bogdan offered himself not once, but twice, and still returned to us alive and well. Surely this is a sign from God. He has a plan, you must believe, if only we might remain patient and allow our Lord in Heaven to conduct his divine work."

The people were not as easily convinced by the priest as Bogdan had been. They wanted little of his ancient Bible stories. The only thing they understood was that the people around them, people they knew and loved, were falling like the trees fell in the forest.

"Who would have been sacrificed?" A faceless voice called out from somewhere deep within the crowd. "Who was next in line for the ceremony?"

"Ilya," said another voice. "It was Ilya's time to die so that the rest of us might live."

"Please!" The priest waved his arms in the air as he tried to regain control. It was useless. Whatever he said was drowned in a turbulent sea of voices.

Within minutes it was settled. The ceremony would resume without delay. That it was not the customary date, or that the priest refused to lead them, mattered not. The only thing that mattered, they decided together in the feverish way an angry mob often decides things, was that the boy would be sent to his death that very night.

Ilya kicked and screamed as they tore him away from the arms of his mother and father.

Torches were lit. Words were spoken. And then, when he'd been fastened to the tree with the same leather cords that had once bound Bogdan's hands, he was left alone for the evil spirit.

Bogdan could only imagine what the terrified, gentle boy was thinking. The poor boy, who had lived his whole life beneath the specter of death, and who'd been spared from the same fate as the others by Bogdan's twice-over survival, had full knowledge his end was near, yet no time in which to prepare himself for the violence that would come. It was a terrible way to die.

"It's awful," he said.

Svyatoslav nodded in agreement as he lit his pipe. "I'd give myself in his place if such a thing could be done. But what would the evil spirit want with my dusty old sack of bones?"

Earlier in the day, the priest had disappeared into the church and had not been seen again. Bogdan and Svyatoslav had tried once more to stop the murderous mob. But their desperate pleas and protests fell upon deafened ears. He was no longer Bogdan the Great, just the man who had betrayed them.

Worse yet had been the boy's mother, who'd begged him not to let them proceed. She had to be carried back to the house by Ilya's father, tears washing down her face. It made him sick now, those sorrowful cries which played in his head. There would be no salvation, no miracles, no happy ending. There was nothing left to do but wait.

The mother's cries had been bad enough, but it was young Ilya's torturous wails of horror that kept him awake throughout the night. The boy would not offer himself quietly. Bogdan could only toss and turn in his empty bed before wandering back out into the cool summer night.

More than once, he thought to save the boy, but the villagers kept close watch, the biggest and boldest among them following closely behind as he paced from one end of the village to the other.

"Don't make trouble," they'd said. It would only serve to delay Ilya's grisly end, for they would come to sacrifice the boy one way or another.

Who were they to speak to him in such a way? They were nothing more than cowardly farmers, who until now had been content to let others die in their place while they tended to their sheep and crops.

Perhaps, he thought, Svyatoslav could slip past them and reach the boy. But it was of no use. A visit to the house of his closest friend would not go unnoticed—and even if they were successful in setting the boy free, what then? Where would they take him? And what would stop the villagers, who had tasted blood and would not rest until more had been spilled, from sacrificing another?

He was never more in need of the priest. The old man had shut himself away, too disheartened by the events of the day to attend to the world of men. Surely, thought Bogdan, he would be deep in prayer. But he was desperate for the man's counsel.

He'd just arrived at the steps of the church, a pair of suspicious eyes still trailing behind him, when the boy stopped screaming. Had he simply tired and given up, or had the evil spirit come to accept the village's offer?

Bogdan wasn't going to wait any longer to find out. He ran, the men who had been assigned to watch him in close pursuit, to the old tree where the deadly chain of events were first set in motion—the night he himself had been offered up to the beast.

Young Ilya was still lashed to the tree, his head slumped to one side. Thin lines of blood ran from the boy's ears and eyes and open mouth. Bogdan listened for a breath and heard nothing.

Ilya was dead.

He was tender with the knife as he cut the boy down, supporting his limp body and lowering him gently to the earth. He leaned in close and kissed him on the forehead. He wanted to feel anger, to curse the villagers for what they had done, but it would only dishonor the life of a sweet and gentle boy, who in his short years among them, was known for his innocent smile and the love he'd had for his mother.

Daylight had just begun to break when he took the boy's body in his arms and carried him to the place in the center of the village where they'd built a makeshift funeral pyre. Ilya's mother, supported by her husband, was the first to arrive. She sobbed again, heavy tears falling to the dirt, as she wiped the blood from the boy's face and ran her fingers through his blonde hair. "He was so beautiful," she said. "I pray he is with our Lord God in Heaven."

"I'm sorry," said Bogdan. He knew it was not enough. There were no words which might cure the pain a mother felt at the loss of her child. He was only glad his own dear mother, who'd only recently retired with his father to the village where she'd been born, was not there to share in the grieving woman's agony.

As the the sun broke over the horizon, more villagers came to assemble at the place where Bogdan had brought young Ilya's body to its final rest. They spoke in hushed tones and thanked God the spirit had accepted their offering. Things would go back to normal, they whispered. They had only done what they should have done from the very beginning. The only shame, they said, was that the others had to die first.

Bogdan loathed them. He stood on the edge of the clearing and watched them deliver bold assurances that they had in fact done the right thing. But he knew the priest was right. It was they who had traded their faith in God for a deal with the Devil. He decided in that moment he would take his son and leave the village. There had to be a place, he imagined, where people would not sacrifice their neighbor out of fear.

"Fools!" A voice washed over the crowd and silenced them. It was the priest, who had finally emerged from the sanctuary of the church. His hair and robes were disheveled. He had the look of a man who had not slept. "The Devil rejoices, for while you might live this day and the next, he has claimed your very souls for all eternity."

His speech was met with boos and jeers. What did they care for the ramblings of a tired old priest? He had betrayed them, they said, along with the man who would forever be remembered as Bogdan the Terrible.

Someone lit a torch. The boy's body was lifted above their heads and tossed upon the pyre. A roaring fire erupted, and the people cheered. They would celebrate with a great feast, for surely now the evil spirit had been appeased.

Their joyous mood was soon shattered by a single scream. It had come from a house at the far end of the village, and was joined not long after by another. Then another. The crowd panicked—the flames of Ilya's funeral pyre were reflected in their wide eyes like the fires of Hell.

"My husband!" A woman stumbled from one of the nearby houses and collapsed to the ground at the feet of the priest. "My poor husband is dead!"

He wasn't the only one. By morning's end, the number of dead totaled seven—three men and four boys—each discovered, like the others, cold and lifeless in their beds.

The sacrifice of young Ilya was in vain. The evil spirit had sent a message. He wouldn't stop, not until every last one of them had perished.

SEVENTEEN

The old woman had turned out to be an excellent nanny. While Nancy was happy to have so much help with Nora, she'd grown bored at the days spent wasting away in the house. It wasn't supposed to be like this, she thought. She should be wining and dining with the women she'd once called friends, but her husband's legal troubles had destroyed any hope she had of returning to the inner circles of Boston's high society.

In the weeks and months since his arrest, more of his former clients had come forward to accuse him of stealing their life savings. With each new victim, the media coverage was renewed.

She'd gaped in horror the first time she saw her name printed beside his in the New York Times. There was even a photo of her at one of the charity banquets she'd once been so keen to attend. No doubt one of her former friends had been paid good money for it. The only positive was the black dress she'd worn—at least no one could accuse of her of being a slouch.

Her only choice was to pass most days in bed, a bottle of sleeping pills on the nightstand within easy reach. They were the only thing that gave her some comfort. Once, on a particularly fine afternoon, she finally worked up the courage to venture out into the garden, but the whirring rotors of a news helicopter flying overhead sent her scurrying back into the house.

Mr. Hardaway was poor company. He spent his days prepping for the trial with his good-for-nothing lawyer. He'd go into the study and close the door, and when he finally emerged late in the evenings, he'd trudge up to bed without saying a word.

If it wasn't for Inez she'd be totally alone. They were taking coffee together in the kitchen when there was an unexpected knock on the front door.

"Don't worry," said the housekeeper. "I'll take care of it."

Nancy had grown tired of the interruptions. It was always some reporter with a camera in tow. None of them were interested in anything she had to say. They'd shout accusations and get their ten-second video clip for the evening news. She'd begged Byron to hire a security firm to post someone outside, but as she'd grown accustomed to hearing over the weeks and months leading up to the trial, there were no funds for such a frivolous expense. Inez, for her part, had been diligent in sending them away. They had no use for a video clip of the housekeeper.

Nancy listened from the kitchen as the no-nonsense woman closed the door in yet another reporter's face. If she could, she would have given her a raise.

"I'm sorry," she said, when Inez returned to the kitchen. "It's not your job to handle media relations."

Inez laughed. "It's no trouble, Mrs. Hardaway."

Nancy had always considered herself superior the other woman. She was the employer, after all, and the dispensing of paychecks brought with it a certain power. But her fall from grace had bestowed a sense of humility. There were moments when she admired Inez for her honesty and her unshakeable dedication to her own family. "Please," she said, "it's about time you started calling me Nancy."

The housekeeper's face knotted up as if she were solving a difficult puzzle. "You sure, Mrs. Hardaway?"

"Yes, Inez. I'm quite sure. You're such a wonderful presence in our home. We can't possibly do enough to thank you."

"Okay, Nancy." The name slipped between her lips with some degree of difficulty. "I appreciate your kind words. If only those reporters knew what a nice lady you were, maybe they'd stop bothering us."

"They won't stop—not until all of this is over. Even then, I'm not sure things will ever go back to normal."

"Have faith, Nancy. Put your trust in God and let him lead the way. He'll carry you out of this mess."

God. She'd always secretly balked at the woman's religious convictions. It seemed to her like nothing more than a folly for those too weak to make their own way in life. She'd always gotten along just fine, she told herself often, without any help from God. But maybe Inez was right. Besides, with Byron's trial starting soon, she was going to need all the help she could get.

It was an awful affair. Day after day she passed through a set of metal detectors, sour-faced court officers waving her down with a wand like a common criminal whenever she forgot to remove some piece of jewelry. Then there was the courtroom itself, with the judge presiding over everything like some kind of feudal lord.

She tried to smile at him once. It would do good to make a positive impression on the man who held her husband's fate—and by extension her own fate—in his hands. But the black-robed man was entirely without expression, a general look of disdain for her husband and the details of his trial the only exception.

She was in enemy territory. All around her, crowded into the long rows of wooden benches, were the families of those who had been fleeced. She caught their sideways looks— their eyes burning into the back of her head. Every torturous minute in that room passed like an eternity.

The jury selection came first and lasted a full two days. Potential jurors were questioned by the prosecutor and Mr. Bennett about their backgrounds, their families, and whatever knowledge they might have about the case.

"I hope he burns in hell," said a rough looking man who spoke of hardworking families and the retirement savings which had been lost to her husband's scheming. "It's people like you," he said, addressing her husband directly, "who get rich on the backs of people like me."

While the prosecution had been keen to see the angry man selected to the jury, Mr. Bennett made quick work of having him dismissed. Still, there was only so much damage control the beady-eyed lawyer could do.

There were very few who hadn't heard at least something about the case, a handful of odd types and modern day recluses, who would eventually form the committee of twelve that would decide her husband's innocence or guilt.

The whole thing seemed rather improbable, and yet there she was at the center—the balance of everything coming down to the will of a dozen strangers. She remembered something Inez had said about leaving judgement to God. It was beginning to make a lot of sense.

On the third day, the trial was set to begin. They'd arrived early so Nancy could take up a position directly behind Byron, who sat alongside his lawyer at the same table where he'd sat during the preliminary hearing. She fidgeted on the hard wooden bench and stood when the room was called to order.

The prosecutor, a tall, grey-haired man in a cheap, ill-fitting suit, was first to give his opening statement.

"Your Honor, ladies and gentleman of the jury, as I stand before you today I'm filled with disappointment." He let each word hang for dramatic effect like a bad actor in a second-rate theater performance. "While the facts of this case are clear, there will be no winner. The victims of this well-planned and carefully orchestrated crime have, in many cases, lost their entire life savings. Can you imagine, everything they've worked so hard to achieve, decades of sacrifice and disciplined effort, lost in the blink of an eye to the greed of a single man?

"That man is Byron James Hardaway." He pointed to her husband with a shaky finger. "Mr. Hardaway also stands to lose everything—his stolen money, his life of luxury, and even his very freedom. This is truly a sad day for everyone.

"But I must do my duty," he said, turning to face the jury. "And you must do yours. Over the coming days and weeks, you will challenged with the complexities of a bold financial scheme designed only to mislead, misdirect, conceal, and steal from those who put their trust in the man now seated before you. It will not be easy, but I will do my best to present the government's case with clarity and precision. I ask only one thing, that when the facts of this case have been presented, and the defendant's crimes have been revealed, you, in your civic duty as the members of this jury, convict this man and send him away to prison. It's only right. It's what he deserves."

Nancy drifted off as the man continued to speak. It was all so terribly boring, not at all like the legal dramas she'd watched on television. There were no sexy lawyers, no striking sound effects as they cut quickly from scene to scene. She hardly noticed when the prosecutor finished speaking and her husband's lawyer took his turn at the front of the room.

"Members of the jury, the prosecutor has presented a strong emotional appeal. He would have you believe my client is nothing more than a monster, stealing candy from the mouths of babies in order to satisfy his unending greed. But what about the facts? Do they not matter? Ladies and gentleman, your time is valuable, so I'll keep it short."

Thank goodness, she thought. Another long speech might have put her to sleep.

"My client is not a monster. The man before you is a loving husband and devoted father. He didn't steal from anyone. Like the prosecutor, I have one request—that as this trial unfolds you consider only the cold, hard facts. And as the facts will surely demonstrate, this is nothing more than a few instances of misguided accounting and unfortunate, but inevitable downturns in the market. People invest. Sometimes they win. Sometimes they lose. To place the blame entirely on the shoulders of a single man is not only wrong, it's un-American."

After months of bad press, she was glad to finally hear someone defending her poor husband, but she could have done without the last part. It was a touch over-the-top to resort to patriotic dogma, though one of the jurors had nodded along as Mr. Bennett made his final point.

"We only need a single dissenter," the lawyer had explained to her a week before, as they made final preparations for the trial. "It's unrealistic to think Mr. Hardaway will be found innocent. But an acquittal is just as good at keeping him out of prison."

She was beginning to feel a sliver of hope when a flurry of shouting and activity erupted near the front of the courtroom. She turned just in time to see a young woman—the same young woman who'd stalked her after the preliminary hearing—leap over the low, wooden railing and make a desperate grab for a court officer's holstered pistol.

The officer, who'd been caught off guard by the young woman's surprise leap for his sidearm, composed himself just in time to help his partner drive the woman down to the ground.

A shot rang out.

The spectators and media who had been crowded into the gallery pressed against each other as they started toward the door in a single wave. The old judge, despite his advanced age and generally fragile appearance, was quick to duck behind the raised bench.

Nancy had little time to react. She could only watch the scene unfold as if it was happening in some distant place, far removed from the mind-numbing events of the day.

It was over just as soon as it had started. The bullet had struck a ceiling tile, nothing more, and the woman was wrestled into a pair of handcuffs.

"You killed him!" She screamed and fought as they pushed back the crowd and pulled her toward the exit. "That man killed my husband!"

Nancy wanted to throw up. Whatever hope she'd felt only a few short moments before evaporated when she saw the looks of horror on the shocked faces of the jury. The judge called the room back to order and instructed them to ignore what they'd seen, but she knew it was too late. Some things can never be unseen.

The media caught wind of the young woman's stunt and descended on the courthouse in a frenzy. Nancy and Byron sat in frozen silence as the driver of their hired sedan navigated a maze of microphones and cameras. Not even the dark tint of the windows could shield them from the photographers who flung themselves at the car, determined to get their money shots.

Until that moment, she'd never really taken the whole thing seriously. It was just a minor brush with the law. The only real downsides were the negative consequences it had taken on her otherwise thriving social life. But the woman's mad grab for an officer's gun, along with the opening statement by the prosecuting attorney, pierced the delicate veil she'd carefully draped over any doubts which had crept into her mind.

Mr. Bennett, seated up front next to the driver, was the first to speak. "I'm not sure what to say. In all my years as a trial attorney, I've never witnessed anything quite like that."

It was hardly the reassurance she'd been hoping for. "What impact will this have on the trial?"

"Not much." The lawyer twisted around in his seat and gripped the back of the leather headrest. "If your husband is found guilty, I might be able to request a new trial. There's certainly a strong case to be made for jury interference. But I can't imagine the current judge calling for a new jury selection this late in the game."

Guilty. It was the one word she tried the hardest not to think about. The thought of being alone in that empty house, with nothing but the baby and a couple of old women, sent shivers down her spine. She imagined herself like Penelope, gazing out longingly over the water as she waited for Odysseus to return. But her life was not an epic Greek poem, and Byron was certainly not Odysseus.

They arrived at the house to find another throng of vans lining the street, their respective news crews buzzing about. The neighbors, who in previous months had appeared on their front stoops to drink coffee and watch the calamitous spectacle, were nowhere to be seen. They're too busy scheming and devising a plan to run us out of the neighborhood, she thought, for all the trouble we've brought them.

"Nancy!" A reporter pressed in close and waved a microphone in her face as she exited the black sedan. "What do you think about the accusations made by the woman in the courtroom?"

She knew better than to say anything, but she couldn't restrain herself. "You mean the woman who pulled a gun and put a bullet through the ceiling? I'm not sure she's fit to be making accusations about anyone."

"She claims your husband, Mr. Hardaway, stole all of their money, and that her own husband, faced with the pressure of losing their house, killed himself out of desperation. What do you have to say about that?"

Mr. Bennett stepped between them before Nancy had another chance to respond. "What happened today was nothing more than a violent, criminal act. I salute the fine law enforcement officers who were quick to respond with such bravery and professionalism. This is a matter for the district attorney, not my client. We have no further comments at this time."

Inez ushered them in through the front door and was quick to close it behind them. It was some time before the chaos finally subsided and the lawyer slinked away. Nancy, with nothing to do and nowhere to go, dropped herself to the leather sofa in Mr. Hardaway's study.

"Listen," he said. "I know this has all been very difficult for you. I'm sorry."

"What are we going to do, Byron?" She was too numb to cry. Her thoughts had given way to emptiness.

Beyond the window of the study, in the small space between the house and the reporters who were still gathered on the street, the caretaker's son bounced a ball on the sidewalk, perfectly oblivious to the chaos. She watched his blonde hair bob up and down with the rhythm of the ball, and for a moment she was jealous. It would be wonderful, she thought, to be so innocent again, if only for a day.

Her husband's voice snapped her attention back to the heavy, wood-paneled room. "Mr. Bennett says the evidence is in our favor, and I believe him. We have to be patient, Nancy. It's all we can do."

"Mr. Bennett charges five-hundred dollars an hour. He'll say whatever he thinks you want to hear so long as you continue to make the payments."

Byron lowered his head into his hands. "I'm just trying to stay positive, Nance. Don't you think I'm afraid? I'm the one looking at federal prison. Believe me, if it wasn't for you and the baby I'd be on the next flight to Brazil."

"Well, aren't you a hero?" Blood boiled up beneath her skin as she fought back tears of rage. How could he be such a coward? "Please, don't let a silly little thing like your family stop you. It certainly didn't stop you from stealing that money. If you want to run away then by all means go. We're probably better off without you."

His face twisted up and froze as if she'd reached right out and slapped him. "I'm sorry, Nancy. I shouldn't have said that. I would never abandon you. I would never abandon our beautiful daughter. You're the only thing I have."

As she stared back at his sad eyes, she saw a distant shadow of the young man who'd courted her all those many years ago, naïve but driven, with an ambition that masked the lingering insecurities of a middle class youth. She wanted to hug him, to tell him all had been forgiven. But then she remembered the stern words of her father, who told her that forgiveness was nothing more than a sign of weakness, an opportunity for those who might take advantage of the slightest act of kindness.

"It's getting late." She decided the best way to punish him was to leave him there alone, with only his cognac and regret to keep him company. "I'm going to check on the baby."

She climbed the steps at a brisk pace, but hesitated outside the door of the nursery. It was a regular occurrence, ever since she'd first discovered the body of their former nanny sprawled dead on the floor. It was silly, she told herself. The nanny's untimely death was a one-time event, chalked up to some rare, inexplicable medical condition. Still, entering the nursery always gave her pause.

She'd just steadied herself with a deep breath when she heard a strange noise. It was Nora, that much was obvious, but it was nothing like the familiar cooing and crying sounds which emerged at all hours from her tiny lips.

It was a single word.

"Ree-na."

EIGHTEEN

Cowardly men and women, who only a short time before had condemned him, threw themselves at his feet and begged his forgiveness. Their plan to save the village had failed, and there would be no salvation from the terrible scourge of the evil spirit.

Bogdan the Great—they championed his name once more, as if it might somehow be restored to its former glory—was their last and only hope.

"Please," they said. "You must save us."

He'd spent all morning burying the dead.

Svyatoslav had helped him, fetching a wooden cart from the house of the tinsmith, who would no longer have use for it save for one final ride to his permanent resting place.

They went house by house, taking turns pulling the heavy cart behind them, as they ferried the bodies of those who had perished in the night to the freshly dug graves they'd prepared not long before.

One by one they lowered the bodies into the ground, the priest administering the funeral rites as Bogdan drove a makeshift cross of bound sticks into the soft earth at the head of each grave.

The villagers had been of little use. They passed the hours in collective mourning, huddled together on rough-hewn benches inside the church. Frightened words passed back and forth between their nervous lips. Many spoke of gathering what few possessions they had and fleeing the cursed village before another night fell upon them. Surely, they said, there would be more souls taken. All agreed the evil spirit would not rest.

How Bogdan wanted to condemn them, they who had been so quick to accuse him of treachery, of conspiring with the priest to make a pact with the Devil. It was the priest who convinced him otherwise.

"You must not abandon them now," said the old man.

"No? Tell me why I should stand beside them, for they were unwilling to stand beside me."

"My son, do you not see? Yours is the terrible burden borne throughout history by all great men and women. The people are nothing more than children, hopeless and fickle. As our Savior Jesus Christ forgave those who left him to suf-fer upon the cross, you must now forgive all those who have wronged you."

They didn't deserve his forgiveness. The priest was right about one thing—they were children. They would fight and bicker among themselves until every last one of them had been destroyed. Such was the way of men.

He had every reason, he told himself, to take his son and leave that place. But he knew it would be the same no mat-ter where he might go. Perhaps there would be no evil spirit, but there would be something else. People always found rea-son to tear themselves apart, rather than come together.

Would it really be so different in another village, a bustling city, or a far-flung country? Their village was the only home he'd ever known, and he thought just maybe, despite the evil which appeared to triumph all around him, it was as good a place as any.

"Friends," said the priest, who had taken his usual place at the front of the church. "You have come here to seek sanctuary, and for good reason. Our lands have been plagued for too long, our precious sons and husbands have fallen. And in your most desperate hour, the very Devil himself has tempted you away from the Lord. But hear me now, it is never too late for God's loving forgiveness. Be not weak. Be not the fir bough which bends and breaks beneath the weight of a heavy snow in winter. For one day the trumpets will sound, our spring will come, and we shall again find ourselves in the resplendent light of the Lord."

Their nervous chatter fell silent. All eyes were upon the priest, with his wild hair and disheveled robes. The old man was fighting a battle for their hearts and minds, and he was winning.

They may be as fickle as children, Bogdan thought, but they were also desperate. They were in need of a strong leader, and who else might lead them if not he?

"Good people," said the priest, "your prayers have not gone without answer. For the Lord has sent us a son. He is the only one among us capable of lifting the curse. We must have faith. We must not be lead astray."

He raised his arms one last time over his head, as if he might call down the heavens. "My dear brothers and sisters, I am but a tired priest. I have little more to offer than words. But I implore you, hear my words now. The Lord has heard your prayers and delivered us Bogdan the Great."

The old man dropped his arms and they were left once more in silence. It was the voice of a woman that rose first, drifting in from the back of the church. "Bogdan," she said. "Bogdan the Great!"

Soon her voice was joined by the others, until every last one of them was chanting his name in unison. The priest stepped aside from the pulpit, and it was his turn to address the tired and huddled crowd.

He'd planned no words of his own. Moments ago he'd loathed them, but as he took his place behind the pulpit and stared into their weary eyes, he saw reflected back at him something they'd long-since given up. It was hope—and the strengthened belief that somehow he would save them. But what might he say? It was only when he opened his mouth that the words came, as if arriving at his lips from some distant place.

"I am a simple man," he said. "If you would ask the priest, he would speak of miracles and saviors. I am not a savior, and I know nothing of miracles. Why has this terrible beast cursed us with his presence? Why must our children suffer and pay with their lives? Who among us can say? But of one thing I am certain."

The crowd leaned in, as if he might reveal some great secret. The shaky wooden benches of the church strained beneath their weight. Even the priest had moved closer, an old and wrinkled hand raised to his ear, so that he might hear whatever Bogdan would say next.

"For too long we have waited, tending to our fields in the hope that somehow this evil would abate. It's clear now it will not. And so we cannot wait any longer. We must seek him out, in the very place where his dark spirit lies dormant in the bright light of day. Good people, we must find him, and with our courage and our faith in the Lord we must send his wretched soul back to Hell."

At this they stood, several of the benches toppling over beneath them, as they jumped to their feet and shouted cheers of approval.

"Bogdan is right," said a woman who'd lost both her husband and her son. "We mustn't wait any longer."

"Yes," said another. "We must act now, before the last of us has perished."

Bogdan looked at the priest, standing quietly in his black and ruffled robes. A peculiar expression had taken over the old man's tired face—something which had been unimaginable only hours before. It was a smile.

Bogdan felt renewed. How he would find and destroy the evil spirit was still a question for which he did not yet have an answer. It would be a difficult and dangerous task, no doubt, but it was a risk he would rather take than to stay and dig another grave.

"Very well," he said. "I will leave before sundown. Who will come with me?"

His questioned silenced them. Anxious faces looked from one to another. It was one thing, he knew, to volunteer himself for such a dangerous mission. It was quite another thing to expect the others to go so willingly.

He'd almost given up hope when the first volunteer stepped forward.

It was Svyatoslav.

"I will go," said the big man. "I would follow you, Bogdan the Great, to the Gates of Hell."

Svyatoslav's son, rarely a man of words, stepped forward to join him. "As would I," he said. "Wherever you lead, Bogdan the Great, I will follow."

They were a fair enough search party, and would do well to travel light. But it was the last volunteer, a young boy not much older than fourteen or fifteen, who he'd not expected to stand up.

"I will go," said the boy, as he stepped forward to take his place beside the two men, much larger than himself, who had already joined Bogdan at the front of the room.

"No, Vladislav." The boy's mother wiped tears from her eyes and pulled at his shirt. "We buried your only brother this very morning. I will not bury a second child."

"Yes," said the boy. He kissed her hand and returned it gently to her side. "That is why I must go, for if I do nothing but wait here I will surely die."

"It's settled," said Bogdan. "Gather your things and say your goodbyes. We leave before the last ray of sun has departed the sky."

The whole of the village, at least those among them who still lived, worked together to prepare the search party. Food and supplies were gathered, along with four sturdy horses, normally reserved for ploughing the fields, which had been volunteered for their journey.

The priest begged to join them, but Bogdan insisted he remain behind. "You're too old," he said. "Who will carry you when your bones bend and break? My friend, you should be here to watch over the village."

"Very well," said the priest. "It's true. I'm an old, simple man. Who am I to argue with Bogdan the Great?"

Bogdan returned the smile the priest had given him in the church. "Come now, father. We both know you're much more than that. You're a true servant of the Lord, and the people will surely have need of your steady heart and mind before the worst of it has passed."

"Go with God, my friend. May His light never fail to guide you through the darkness."

The sun had almost taken its place below the horizon when they set out together, four brave souls in search of an end to the curse which had plagued their people for so many generations.

They rode in silence, the trees closing in around them as they advanced deeper into the forest. A thick canopy of leaves and branches blocked the light of the moon and stars, and the path—nothing more than a thin line of dirt cutting a trail through the heavy underbrush—would have been lost to them had Bogdan not stopped to light a torch.

It must have been midnight, at least it was close by their best guess, when the trail widened and emptied into a small clearing. Svyatoslav urged his horse forward to join Bogdan at the front of the group.

"Fine night for a ride." The big man lit his pipe with a stick held to the torch and took a puff before passing it.

Bogdan picked at a small cut on his cheek, left by a branch which had scratched him in the dark. "Thank you for coming, my friend. The journey would not be the same without you."

"I meant what I said. I'd follow you anywhere. Still, I can't help but wonder where we're going."

It was the same question he'd been considering since his announcement in the church. The words had come without warning. The decision to leave had been made with no time to make a plan.

"Trust your gut," the priest had said.

He took a puff from the pipe and passed it back. "Do you remember the legend—the story told by the priest on the eve of every sacrifice?"

"How could I forget? I've heard it year after year since I was a boy."

"So we follow the legend, back to the place where it all began." He raised a hand and pointed into the distance. A row of mountains loomed low and heavy before them, their dark peaks outlined by the absence of stars.

"It's a long way," said his friend. "It won't be easy to cross the mountains. There are bears, and wolves, and fast running rivers."

"Have we not faced worse?"

Svyatoslav took another puff as he considered. "Indeed we have, though it's not the bears or wolves or rivers that should give us pause. You're too young to remember, but in the summer before you were born, there arrived in our village a band of travelers who had passed through the very same mountains. Whatever supplies they'd managed to carry with them had been taken, along with a half dozen of their women and children. Those who survived spoke of outlaws who set upon them in the night."

"Fear not, dear Svyatoslav. I too, have heard the stories. But the travelers had neither your fine company, nor the company of your brave son. We should not go so far only to fall at the hands of men."

The big man snorted and took another puff. "They didn't have Bogdan the Great. But what of the village? I fear for their safety in our absence."

"Our only hope is to lead the evil spirit away, that he might take notice and follow us over the mountains."

"But will he follow?" Svyatoslav glanced over his shoulder as though he expected to see something.

"Yes," said Bogdan. "He follows us now. I can feel his malevolent presence, watching and stalking close behind like a pale shadow in the night."

NINETEEN

She was somewhere in the dark. Was it the house, or someplace else? She couldn't be sure. The only thing she knew for certain was that she wasn't alone.

It came to her like a shadow, pressing itself against her body as she struggled to wrest herself free. She felt no fear. It was only a game of cat and mouse, like two lovers locked in a passionate tango. When she could resist no longer, she gave herself to the shadow with complete abandon, ripples of pleasure coursing through her body as they joined together in sexual union.

"Nancy." A voice called to her from somewhere far off in the distance.

She didn't want to answer. She wanted to stay there forever in the shadow's erotic embrace.

"Nancy." The voice came again. She felt a touch upon her shoulder, something cold and foreign.

Her eyes opened to find Byron standing over her with a dopey expression on his face.

"You were dreaming," he said.

"What time is it?" She wished he would have let her continue to sleep. Every morning it was the same—they woke up early and got dressed before dodging a sea of reporters on their way to the courthouse. Afternoons were filled with dry testimony, facts and figures she didn't want to understand. By the time they finally made it home in the evenings, she was exhausted. It had been weeks since the trial began, but to Nancy it felt like a lifetime.

"Almost eight." Byron stood before the mirror and fumbled with his tie. "Inez made crêpes for breakfast, blueberries and caramel, and Iryna brought Nora down from the nursery."

She'd said nothing to the old nanny about what she'd heard in the hallway outside the nursery. She was hardly a sentimental woman. What did it matter if Nora's first word wasn't 'mommy' or 'daddy?' Still, it stirred within her an uneasy feeling she couldn't name. Was it simply jealousy, or something closer to guilt?

"The car will be here in forty-five minutes. I hung a dress for you on the closet door."

How sorry her life had become, that her husband, a man totally lacking in style were it not for her meticulous direction, took it upon himself to choose what she might wear. "I'm not going."

"We've been over this, Nancy. Mr. Bennett says it looks better with you there. Juries are more likely to side with a family man. You really should bring Nora."

Nancy imagined the press shoving their cameras in her daughter's face. She might not love Nora the same way other mothers loved their daughters, but she wasn't about to make a spectacle out of her. "I don't care what Mr. Bennett says."

"Please, Nancy. I can't do this alone."

She said nothing as she rolled out of bed. There wasn't time to do her makeup, but it didn't matter. She'd become good at doing it in the car.

Inez and Iryna were waiting in the kitchen. Baby Nora sat in a highchair at the breakfast table, a dab of whip cream hanging from her tiny chin.

Even Nancy, miserable as she was at the prospect of another day in the courtroom, had to admit the baby looked especially cute. Nora giggled a little when she planted a kiss on her soft forehead.

She'd only half-finished her coffee when the driver called to say he'd arrived. "We'll take the crêpes to go, Inez. I'm afraid my husband is expected to be punctual."

"Of course, Nancy." The housekeeper still hesitated when she called her by her first name. Old habits were tough to kick. "Your lunch is still in the fridge—caprese salad—I wanted to keep the tomatoes fresh. Oh, and I packed one of those chocolates you love."

"What would I do without you?" It was more than a rhetorical question. Two days before, she'd thrown a small fit when Byron suggested cutting another member of the household staff. If only it was a decision between her husband and Inez. She would gladly choose the housekeeper.

Security had been stepped up at the courthouse in the wake of the desperate woman's grab for a court officer's gun. Nancy feigned a smile as the security staff combed through her personal belongings. Mr. Bennett had cautioned her not to say anything, but in her not-so-humble opinion the extra measures had become too ridiculous to tolerate. She couldn't help herself when they insisted on picking through the lunch Inez had so carefully packed. "Be careful," she said. "There's a bomb wedged in between the tomatoes."

The joke did not go over well. A particularly large and sour-faced officer pulled her out of line for a secondary search, along with a stiff admonition from the security supervisor. By the time they'd finished, she was one of the last to arrive at the courtroom, and had to settle for a place between a reporter she recognized from the daily feeding frenzies outside her home, and a woman whose three snot-nosed kids wouldn't stop staring at her.

She'd grown surprisingly accustomed to the gawking of strangers, and gave them little thought as the hours dragged on. Her only real grievance, besides the unending boredom, was the wooden bench. It was some sick form of torture, she thought, to make people sit on hard slabs of wood for eight hours.

It was only after lunch, when she'd eaten the caprese salad and chocolate alone at a small table in the courthouse cafeteria, that something finally caught her attention.

"Your Honor," said the prosecutor, "the people would like to present additional evidence in this case."

Additional evidence? She wondered what else they might have found to use against her husband.

Mr. Bennett was quick to raise a hand. "Objection, Your Honor. The defense was not informed of any new evidence."

The prosecutor ignored him and continued. "Your Honor, the investigators seized a shredder from the defendant's residence. They've only just finished piecing the documents together this morning. We're prepared to furnish copies to the defense, as required when submitting any new evidence in a criminal proceeding."

Nancy's stomach turned. She remembered what Byron had said, that if they discovered the contents of those documents, his fate was as good as sealed.

The judge called the attorneys for the prosecution and defense to the bench. There were several minutes of hushed discussion before he finally ruled. "Very well. The court will admit the new evidence. These proceedings are adjourned until Monday in order to allow the defense an adequate period for review."

The prosecutor's thin, hollowed-out face stretched into a grin.

"It's bullshit," the lawyer said on the ride back to the Hardaway's home. "They've had those documents all along, waiting until just the right moment. How could the judge fall for such an obvious farce?"

Nancy struggled to understand. "Can they do that?"

"I'm afraid they just did."

Her husband had been silent for much of the car ride home. She'd almost forgotten about him—her attention focused on the lawyer—when she felt his hand on her knee.

"I'm sorry," he said. "I'm sorry for everything."

They dropped her off at the front door. She watched from a curtained window as the black sedan sped away in the direction of Mr. Bennett's downtown office. Byron had gone with the lawyer. At least she wouldn't have to spend another afternoon in that dreadful courtroom.

Inez and the old nanny were helping themselves to hot tea in the kitchen. "You're home early," said the housekeeper. "Is everything okay?"

Okay was a relative term, she thought, as she joined them at the table. The new evidence was concerning, but she was sure the lawyer would work something out. The very real possibility of her husband going to prison was something she tried her best not to consider.

"You look exhausted," said the nanny. "Have some tea. It's chamomile, quite soothing for the nerves."

"Does it show?" She raised her slender fingers to her face and felt for wrinkles. "It's just this trial—Byron has me up early every morning."

"Don't fret, dear. I'm quite certain your youthful vigor will return just as soon as this is behind you. Have you been sleeping well?"

She was reminded of her dream. It wasn't the first time the shadowy stranger had visited her in the night. Perhaps it was nothing more than unfulfilled sexual urges. Byron wasn't much use in bed in the months since he'd returned home from jail. Still, she wasn't about to discuss her sex life, or lack thereof, with the two women seated at the table. "Oh, I've been sleeping well enough."

"Wonderful," said the old woman as she poured herself another cup of tea. "There's nothing more unsettling to one's constitution than a bad night's sleep."

Nancy wondered if there was something more to the nanny's questions. Iryna had made no complaints in her time with the Hardaways, and as far as Nancy could tell, was free of the terrible nightmares which had inflicted the others. If the old woman had indeed suffered the same fate, there were no screams in the night to serve as evidence. Still, she was curious as to why Iryna was so resilient. "Forgive my terrible manners," she said. "I've been so preoccupied with the trial, I forgot to ask if your room is adequate."

"No apology required, Mrs. Hardaway. Everything is quite adequate, and Inez has done a splendid job helping me get settled."

"Yes, I'm afraid nothing would ever get done around here if it wasn't for Inez's efforts. Is the mattress okay? We should have replaced it ages ago."

Iryna dropped a spoonful of sugar in her tea and stirred. "No need to trouble yourself. I'm from a long line of rugged stock—I could sleep soundly on a pile of rocks. But if you mean to ask whether I've been having the same nightmares as your previous nannies, I can assure you I have not."

"How do you know about the other nannies?" Nancy shot a quick glance to Inez. Perhaps the housekeeper had made mention of it. Though the two women had hardly become friends, they had made a regular habit of taking tea together.

Iryna smiled. "Boston may seem like quite a large city to the casual observer, though you know as well as anyone it functions more like a small town. In fact, it was the untimely death of your first nanny, and the rumors which circulated not long after, that led me to your door. A good nanny always has her ear to the ground."

Nancy blushed. "I should have said something that night when you came around."

"It's quite alright, dear. I've no belief in creatures that go bump in the night. And as for that poor young girl, I'm sure it was nothing more than an undiagnosed medical condition. I only wish it hadn't happened so near the baby. Now why don't you have a nice, hot bath? I'll head upstairs and draw the water while you finish your tea."

When they could hear the water running upstairs, Inez leaned in close. "I still don't trust her, Nancy."

"Oh? I thought you two were getting along nicely."

"I'm watching her," said the housekeeper. "I won't let anything happen to you or the baby."

Inez had always been cautious. Sometimes a little too cautious. But Nancy was touched by the woman's unending devotion. "Wouldn't you agree things have been more settled with Nora since Iryna arrived?"

"Oh, yes," she said. "I have no doubt. It's just that something about her doesn't sit right."

"Could you be more specific?" Nancy trusted Inez, perhaps more than she trusted anyone, and was curious about what she might have to say.

"Well, on Mondays some of the local housekeepers meet to do our grocery shopping together. It's kind of a little club we put together—a girl's day out."

She found it rather amusing, the idea of so many fussy housekeepers all shopping together in one place. She could only imagine the juicy gossip that traded lips as the women picked and squeezed fresh produce. "What does that have to do with the nanny?"

"Forgive me, Nancy. I know it's not appropriate to involve myself in your business, but I asked some of the other housekeepers what they know about Iryna."

"And?"

"That's the strange thing. None of them had ever heard of her before. Believe me when I tell you these women know practically everything."

Nancy couldn't help but agree. If you wanted to know what happened behind closed doors in Boston, you need only ask the housekeepers. But whatever doubts she had about the nanny were far outweighed by the woman's tender and able care for Nora. She wasn't about to lose the help, especially not while Byron's trial occupied every minute of her day. "Couldn't it be possible she worked on the other side of town? I'm sure there are quite a lot of nannies over in Cambridge."

"What did it say on her résumé?" The housekeeper suddenly look very embarrassed, as if she'd overstepped her bounds by asking the question.

"I don't recall," said Nancy. "Byron usually looks into those things."

"I see."

The sound of water running in the upstairs bathroom disappeared. Nancy finished the last of her tea. "Please excuse me, Inez. I'm so terribly exhausted and a hot bath is just what I need."

"Of course. You're under so much stress, and the last thing I want to do is add more. I wouldn't have said anything if I didn't think it was worth saying."

"It's quite alright, Inez." She placed a hand on the housekeeper's arm. "Your concern for Nora is touching. I'll be sure to ask Byron about Iryna's work history just as soon as he returns home. I'm sure it's nothing more than a misunderstanding."

She thought about what Inez had said as she climbed the stairs and slipped into her robe. She had no intention of speaking with her husband. It was he who had tasked her with checking the nanny's references. Inez was only being paranoid. The Greater Boston area was home to some five million people, and while the housekeepers of Beacon Hill were certainly well informed, they could hardly track the activities of an entire city.

Nevertheless, as she slid into the hot bath—Iryna had scented the water with lavender and placed a lit candle on a shelf beside the tub—she couldn't shake a nagging feeling of doubt. It was as if Inez's suspicions, as overblown as they might be, had infected her mind like a virus. As she sunk deeper into the water, she knew there was only one thing she could do to put her mind at ease.

She was still in her bathrobe as she tiptoed down the stairs and into Byron's study. The old woman's résumé was right where she had left it, crumpled up in a bottom drawer littered with various documents left behind after the raid.

Her heart sank when she read the first reference. It was not, as she had hoped, a well-to-do family from Cambridge, or even out in Amherst, but an address in Back Bay, not more than a mile from the Hardaway's home. While she didn't recognize the name, Inez's gaggle of housekeepers would have likely known if Iryna had in fact been employed there for the ten years listed on her résumé.

A knot grew in her stomach as she fired up the tablet on Byron's desk and typed the address into the search bar. It didn't take long to find the public property records. The knot in her stomach jumped to her throat when she read the name listed on the official record. She checked the résumé twice to be sure it wasn't a mistake.

The names didn't match.

An abrupt knock on the study door sent her heart racing. Her fingers trembled as she stashed the crumpled piece of paper back in the bottom drawer. "Who is it?"

The door slid open and Iryna entered, a smile on her wrinkled old face. "I went to check on you in the bathroom and you'd disappeared."

"Yes," she said, trying to smooth the nervous cracks in her voice. "I remembered something Byron had asked me to look over. It couldn't wait."

"Is everything alright, Mrs. Hardaway?" The smile left her face. "You look like you've just seen a ghost."

Perhaps that's what the old woman was, she thought—a phantom, a ghost. It would certainly explain her sudden appearance on their doorstep at the exact stroke of midnight. That particular detail had never sat well with Byron. "It's the trial. I've had a long day."

Whatever tension had accumulated in the room was broken by the distant cries of the baby, drifting down from the nursery.

"I understand, dear. You must try to get some rest. I'll go check on Nora."

"Iryna, one last thing before you go." She wanted to stop her, this woman, this ghost, who stood before her now like a stranger. She wasn't sure it was safe for her to be around the baby, at least not until they'd cleared up any confusion about her résumé. But she thought it would be unwise to confront her without Byron present. Who could say what the old woman might do?

"Yes?"

"Thank you," she said. "Thank you for everything."

TWENTY

The men were tired. Bogdan could see it plainly on their haggard faces. It had been two weeks since they first left the village, and although they were exhausted, not once had they uttered a complaint.

They'd slept little, riding at night and taking only a few hours rest by day—one of them always remaining awake to stand guard and roust the others before the last light of day sank behind the mountains. It wasn't easy, sleeping in shifts beneath the bright, summer sun, but it was the only way to protect themselves from the beast who followed them through the dark.

Bogdan was already awake when Vladislav came to roust him. Any doubts he still had about the youngest among them vanished when, that very night, the pack containing their dried meat came loose and fell during a precarious river crossing.

It was the boy who threw himself headfirst into the swiftly moving current. Bogdan thought he might be carried away to drown, but Vladislav emerged soon after on the riverbank, a smile spreading across his face as he clutched the waterlogged pack against his chest.

The meat, though a bit soggy, had been saved, and they cheered his courage as they stripped the clothes from his shivering body and warmed him beside a fire.

"That was fun," he said, his teeth still chattering behind blue lips.

Svyatoslav was the first to laugh, followed soon after by his son. Even Bogdan, serious as he was, laughed until his belly ached. He couldn't remember the last time he'd laughed like that. Maybe, he thought, it had been with Yekaterina.

When the boy stopped shivering, and his clothes were sufficiently dry, they carried on again into the night. The trail wound up and over a narrow pass, and when they came to the other side they saw in the dusty, early morning light the clustered stone houses of a tiny village, not unlike their own.

"I don't like it," said Svyatoslav. "There's not a trace of fire. No chickens. Not even a pig."

"Maybe they bring the chickens in at night." A more natural hue had finally returned to Vladislav's thin and youthful lips. "Were you not the one who said these mountains are home to many wolves?"

Svyatoslav nodded silently.

None of them had been so far south before, not even Svyatoslav, who in his younger days had been a soldier and served many long campaigns in the west. Soon they would cross into the land called Transylvania, a place they knew only from stories and legends.

"It's almost morning," said Bogdan. "We'll need a place to sleep. Perhaps the people of this village are still of our own kind, and would offer us food and shelter from the sun. What have we to fear from a handful of huts?"

Svyatoslav snorted as was his custom when he had nothing to say. They rode together side-by-side, and as they entered the village all was quiet, save for the sound of their horses.

"Hello." Bogdan was the first to speak.

He was answered by the hoot of an owl, somewhere off in the distance.

Vladislav rode up beside him. "Maybe the people are still in their beds."

It would be strange, he thought, for villagers to sleep past dawn. In such a place there was always work to be done —crops to be tended and sheep to be shepherded.

"Hello," he said again.

Svyatoslav had already dismounted and was having a look around. A shepherd's crook leaned against the stone wall of one of the huts. Various tools, the same as one might find in any village, could be seen hanging from hooks beneath the overhangs of thatched roofs.

Though Bogdan was tired, he thought they should ride on and find another place to rest. Although he couldn't say what it was, something about the place made the hair on the back of his neck stand straight.

But young Vladislav, filled with courage from his daring performance at the river, set himself to knocking on doors before Bogdan could stop him. "Hello," he called. "Is anyone here?"

Still, there was no answer. Surely, Bogdan imagined, the boy's knocking would have stirred a pig or chicken. Choosing to ignore his better judgement, he dismounted and joined Vladislav at the door of one of the huts. He fingered the wooden latch and pushed, and was surprised when the door gave way.

Tiny particles of dust, glowing like stars in the night sky, swirled in the beam of light that poured into the dark space of the hut from the open doorway. He waited as his eyes adjusted to the darkness. The first thing he saw was the shape of a long table, dishes and cups strewn about. In opposite corners were two narrow beds. They were empty. The house was abandoned.

It was the same in the rest of the huts. They entered them one by one, and though they found evidence of the lives which had once lived there—a filthy rag-doll, bloodstained cutting boards, even a book or two—there was nothing to suggest the village was occupied.

"It's odd," he said to Svyatoslav. "Where do you think they went?"

Svyatoslav ran his fingers through the wild hair of his coarse beard. "I couldn't say. But it would seem they left in a hurry. Why else would they leave so many of their things behind?"

"They were afraid," he said.

The big man surveyed the forested slopes that closed in all around them. "I don't disagree. But shouldn't we be asking ourselves what frightened them?"

"Bogdan!" Young Vladislav emerged from one of the tiny huts with something in his hands. "Have a look at what I've found."

It was a small piece of slate, the same kind the priest had used to teach Bogdan and the other children of the village how to draw letters like the ones they saw in books. Scrawled upon its rough surface in powdery chalk was a menacing figure, like something drawn from a nightmare.

The sight of it sent a chill traveling down the length of his spine. "Where did you find this?"

Vladislav pointed over his shoulder to the hut. "Just there, under the empty bed. Look closely, there's a word written beneath the figure."

Much to the priest's disappointment, Bogdan had never been good at reading. He struggled to make out the uneven letters of the word. "What does it say?"

"Khyzhak," said the boy. "It means predator."

Svyatoslav surveyed the forest again and ran his fingers over the handle of his axe. "Is it a wolf?"

Bogdan studied the picture. There were arms and legs and a long body, much the same as a man. "It doesn't look like a wolf."

"Then is it the evil spirit? Tell us, dear friend, for you are the only one who has seen him."

"No," he said. "Whatever evil this might be is not the same evil that plagues our village."

"What is it then?"

"A story, a myth, perhaps nothing more. Or maybe it's that which drove these people from their homes with only the clothes on their backs."

"Whatever creature it might be, let us not linger long enough in this place to find out. We should leave at once, Bogdan, and never speak of it again."

"Yes," he said, tucking the strange drawing into his saddle bag. "The horses have had their rest. This is no place to make camp for the day."

And so they continued, eyes burning with the need for sleep, until an hour or two had passed since they left the abandoned village behind them. At last they came upon a small waterfall, and took shelter from the sun in the shade of a rocky outcrop. It was as good a place as any to rest until darkness returned.

"Sleep," he said to his companions. "I'll take the first watch."

Vladislav was the first to nod off. The poor boy hadn't slept since his plunge into the river. Svyatoslav and his taciturn son followed soon after, the sound of their gentle snoring joining together in an offbeat rhythm.

Bogdan found himself alone again, in a place far away from home, though he wondered if he had ever really known the comforts of a home. For a brief moment in time he'd found peace in Yekaterina's arms. He closed his heavy eyes and imagined her face. And then she was with him, beside a waterfall in a strange forest, and he was no longer alone.

A hand on his shoulder jerked him awake. Vladislav stood over him, a grin on his face and a stick of dried meat in his hand.

"You fell asleep," said the boy. "But no harm has been done. There's still another hour of daylight."

Bogdan rubbed his eyes. He was supposed to have kept watch, and was thankful nothing had happened in the time he had been asleep. "Thank you, Vladislav. You've proven your worth yet again."

The boy smiled and nodded toward the others, who still slumbered with their backs against a rock. "Don't worry, I won't say anything."

It was the least of his worries. Most pressing was the evil spirit, who still followed them in the night. Once, when the others were engaged in a lively debate about which of the girls Vladislav should join in marriage, Bogdan caught sight of the beast's red eyes, staring back at him from a distance.

But he was troubled also by the empty village they'd passed through earlier in the day, and the peculiar drawing they'd found beneath one of the beds. As he checked the horses and sent Vladislav to wake father and son, he couldn't shake the feeling that whatever had sent the villagers running was still out there. He hoped only that their paths might never cross.

They set out again not long after dusk. The repose had served them well, and despite the troubling events of the day they were in high spirits.

The trail continued winding its way down from its peak at the pass, and as the forest closed in around them, Svyatoslav whistled an old folk tune.

"Hey, what's that song about?" Vladislav perked up when he heard the melody. "I think my mother used to sing it to me."

"It's about a poor old peasant woman. She sits each day by the window, waiting for her sons to return from a long and distant war. But when they return, much older than when they'd left, the old woman had gone nearly blind and doesn't recognize them."

Vladislav tried whistling the first line. "What happens next?"

"They wait outside the poor old woman's house day after day, until finally the youngest of the sons sings an old folk tune—the very same tune she used to sing to them when they were young. Upon hearing the song, the old woman is overcome with nostalgia and finally recognizes the boys as her own."

"I remember. It's a very famous song."

"Yes," said Svyatoslav. "Mothers sing it to their sons with the hope they might always return."

The two rode along in the dark, boy and man, laughing and whistling, while Bogdan watched the trees. What he was looking for he couldn't be sure, though something in his gut told him the evil spirit wasn't the only thing lurking in the forest.

They'd just crested a small ridge, and arrived at a place where the trail narrowed down to the width of a single horse, when Vladislav's whistle was returned from somewhere in the darkness beyond.

"What was that?" Svyatoslav reached for his axe for the second time in one day.

"Quiet." Bogdan raised a hand to silence him.

A fine mist had fallen over everything, and they could see no farther than a few horse-lengths. They waited together, surrounded by the mist, with only the sounds of the horses stomping and biting at their bits to rupture the uneasy stillness.

A second whistle emerged from the fog, this time from the opposite direction as the first, though Bogdan could only guess from which direction it had truly come.

"Circle the horses," he said. "Whatever happens, we stand together and we fight together."

They had neither sword nor musket. They were not an army, only four tired peasants armed with a hunting bow, a wood-axe, and a pair of hunting knives. But they would not go easily. They had taken up a sacred mission, and whoever might wish to do them harm would need more than luck, for as the priest had said on that evening some weeks ago when they'd set out from the village, they were guided by the Almighty Hand of the Lord.

Soon the first and second whistle were joined by a third, then a fourth. A chorus of whistles—drifting across the fog and bouncing from tree to tree—filled the forest like the sounds of a dispossessed choir.

They couldn't speak. They couldn't move. They could only wait for what might come.

Vladislav was the first to be pulled from his horse, kicking and screaming as a dozen pairs of hands dragged him to the ground and retreated—the boy thrashing about wildly as he disappeared from sight into the heavy mist.

They came for Svyatoslav and his son next. The big man swung his axe and missed, and they were dragged away together through the mud and thick undergrowth.

Bogdan was the last to be pulled from his horse. Black, filthy hands reached and grabbed at him from all directions. He stabbed his knife into the darkness and found flesh. There was blood on the blade but no scream, no cry of agony. A hard blow fell upon his head and the world spun in wobbly circles. The last thing he saw before everything went dark was a strange figure towering over him—half man, half beast.

It was a familiar experience—the headache, the blurred vision, like waking up from a long dream. He tried to move and found he had been tied to a tree. In the light of a nearby fire he could see the others—Vladislav and Svyatoslav, along with his dutiful son. They were bound the same as him, arms pulled back and wrists tied together with leather cords. And there were shadows, others who moved about in the darkness with the bodies of men and the heads of wolves.

"Ah, so you're awake." The largest of the man-beasts squatted down beside him on the soggy earth. He wore no clothing save for a small breechcloth and a pair of boots. His skin was smeared with oil and dirt and reflected the orange glow of the flickering flames.

"Who are you?" Bogdan tried to rub his aching head, but the cords around his wrists held tight.

"You must be the leader. The leader always asks the questions." The man-beast pulled back his mess of fur and teeth to reveal a human face. His eyes were blue, and shone brightly in contrast to his dirty skin. "Did we scare you?"

"We have nothing of value besides the horses," he said. "But you can take them if you let us pass."

"What makes you think you're in a position to negotiate a deal? The last time I checked, it was you tied fast to a tree, not me."

"It's not the first time I've been tied to a tree, or even the second. Yet still I live."

The man-beast grinned, revealing a mouth marked by empty gaps in the places where some of his teeth had once been. He edged closer, and Bogdan smelled the rot on his breath. "Tell me," he said. "What's your name?"

"Bogdan, son of Bogdan."

"Well, Bogdan, son of Bogdan, I'm afraid you and your ragtag band of misfit friends have made a terrible mistake. These mountains belong to us now, and we take whatever we want."

"Is that what happened to the village? Did you take what you want?"

The foul man smiled wider than before. He motioned to one of the others and waited as they fetched a small object from beside the fire. They returned with the chalk slate, and the foul man tossed it at Bogdan's feet. "My name is Yegor," he said. "And it would seem my reputation proceeds me."

Bogdan tried not to imagine the child who must have drawn the picture, terrified and huddled beneath their bed. "Did you kill them?"

"It was a long winter," said Yegor. "We didn't just kill them for sport. We ate them."

So they were true, he thought, the occasional stories that drifted down from the mountains and spread like fire through the villages of the valley. Suddenly it all made sense. He and his companions were nothing more to these wild men than a meal.

He remembered a time when he was only a small boy. His father had taken him into the woods to learn how to set rabbit snares.

"Bogdan," his father had said as he stood over him, "what should you do if you see a bear?"

He was young and foolish then, and had told his father it was best to run.

"No, my son. You should never run from a bear. They can smell your fear."

Afraid as he now was, Bogdan resolved himself not to show this hunter of men his fear, for such a man was no longer human, but a predator, no different from the other predators in the forest. "We've had little to eat ourselves," he said. "I'm afraid we'd make a poor meal. Perhaps you'd prefer to eat the horses?"

Yegor laughed. "You're a clever one, Bogdan. I'm almost beginning to like you. But the horses are much too valuable. We can put them to use. Now, which one of you should we eat first?"

He said nothing. It was not a choice he wanted to make.

"I'm afraid you'll have to decide. It's only right seeing as you're the leader." The foul man shuffled on his heels to the tree where Vladislav was tied. He traced his blackened fingers under the boy's chin. "This one might make a nice meal, if only he wasn't so thin."

"Eat me first." It was the son of Svyatoslav, who had spoken not a single word since their trip began. "Let the boy go and you can eat me this very night."

"I think not, but we'll spare him for now—keep him around until winter and fatten him up. He's rather pretty, like a girl. My men haven't seen a girl in some time. Perhaps they would like to have their way with him."

Vladislav jerked his chin away from Yegor's outstretched hand and spit on the foul man's face—a great wad of phlegm landing squarely on his upper lip.

"Oh, and he's feisty." A long, tattooed tongue emerged from the man's crusty mouth and licked the runny phlegm from his lip. "I like feisty. I might have to keep him for myself."

Bogdan's mind raced as he searched for a way out of what seemed like a hopeless predicament. What would the priest do? He would pray, he thought. The priest would pray. And so he asked the Lord to deliver them from the wicked hands of these men who had become cannibals.

He was almost too distracted to notice the dark figure taking shape beyond the cannibals and the campfire. It was the eyes which caught his attention—bright red eyes which, in his moment of despair, brought with them an uneasy comfort. It was an evil he knew, an evil he understood, an evil from which he would always be beyond reach. And then, as quickly as the eyes had appeared, they vanished, fading back into the blackness of the night.

"You're in luck," said Yegor. "My men have filled their bellies with the meat of a deer and are helping themselves to a cask of fine ale. Even finer was the flesh of the poor merchant from whom we acquired it. They'll have no need of you tonight. Think on your decision, and tell me tomorrow."

Bogdan watched him join the other men beside the fire. They ate and drank and laughed like wild demons, boasting among themselves about who had bedded the prettiest girls. As the night wore on and the moon traced its gentle arc across the sky, they began to fall asleep, one after another, drunk on the ale of a merchant who Bogdan knew would never find his way home.

"Don't sleep," he said to his companions. "Tired as you might be, you mustn't rest your eyes."

"You've seen him?" A thin line of blood ran from Svyatoslav's head. Like Bogdan, he'd been struck during the ambush. "You've seen the evil spirit?"

"Yes, and his insatiable appetite is far greater than that of our captors."

They struggled against the pull of exhaustion until dawn finally broke over the mountains. The wild men were still fast asleep, drunk on the merchant's ale. Bogdan knew it would be some time before they woke.

"Rest now, my friends," he said. "You will need all your strength for what lies ahead."

He had only to close his eyes, and sweet sleep arrived to claim him.

She was with him in his dreams. She was much younger than she'd been the night she died. They were together again in a field of flowers, on that sun-drenched summer day when he'd placed a ring made from the stem of a dandelion on her delicate finger. She laughed and ran her hand through his thick, boyish hair.

"Promise you'll never leave me."

"I'll never leave you," she said. "But you must wake up now, Bogdan. And when this business is finished you must go home."

"I don't want to go home." He began to cry the way he'd only ever cried as a boy. "I want to stay here with you. I'm so very tired. Please, let me stay."

Her hand found its way to his cheek. "My husband, I have made you a promise, and now you must promise me something in return."

"Yes," he said. "What is it you ask? I will promise you anything."

"Promise me that you will be strong, and that you will be a father to our son. He will have need of you."

He would have promised her the moon, but before the words could reach his lips, he was snapped back to the mountains and the forest by a commotion, people shouting in crazed voices around the campsite.

He tore at the bindings on his wrists, but they held firm. "What's happened, Svyatoslav?"

"Who could know?" The big man struggled with his own bindings.

It was some time before the campsite settled. The wild men hovered about in small groups, speaking to each other in hushed tones and whispers. It was strange, Bogdan thought, that there had been no sign of their leader, the man called Yegor. And that's when he saw him, not walking proud and tall as a leader of so many men might, but carried limp and lifeless on a makeshift stretcher. His body was placed beside the fire pit at the center of the campsite, and soon it was joined by five more, just as pale and lifeless as the first.

"Yegor is dead," said one of the wild men. He had a scar across his face and hair as red as flames. Yegor had only just died, and already a new leader had emerged to take his place.

"It was the captives," said a much shorter man, who spit ribbons of saliva from his toothless mouth as he spoke. "They've murdered him."

"Yes," said another. "Let's kill them."

The campsite slid back into chaos. They argued and shouted, until the man who was their new leader slashed the air with a hand in order to silence them. "Very well," he said. "Bring them."

One by one their bindings were cut, and they were dragged, much the same as they had been dragged the night before, to the place where the scarred man stood. Bogdan wondered if they might not all be slaughtered at once, their journey ending in failure almost as soon as it had begun. Was it God's plan that he should be reunited with Yekaterina in death? But he had made her a promise, if only in a dream, to raise their son.

"My people want answers," said the scarred man. "Someone must pay for Yegor's death."

"Did you not cut our bindings with your own hands?" Bogdan scanned the bodies of the dead. There were no wounds upon their flesh. It could have only been the evil spirit who had taken their lives.

The scarred man stroked his chin. "There are those who tell of witches who consort with the Devil. Perhaps it was some dark magic."

He would have denied it, but Vladislav leapt to his feet and spoke first. "Such fools! Do you not recognize the man you have cast in the dirt before you? Have you not heard the stories of Bogdan the Great?"

A whisper passed among them.

"He's not a witch." Vladislav's voice lifted up and carried itself over the crowd. "He's the greatest sorcerer who's ever lived!"

"So it's true," said the toothless wild man. "It was he who killed Yegor."

"Yes, and any man who dares to trespass against him shall discover his vengeful wrath."

Their whispers grew into murmurs, terrified voices debating their next move. There were those who thought it was best to kill them, while others, uncertain whether Bogdan's powers might extend beyond the grave, believed it was too great a chance to take.

In the end, it was the scarred man who spoke for the rest. "Very well," he said. "If you are truly a great sorcerer as you say, then we should like to see one final act of magic. If you succeed, then I shall guide you myself back to the place where we first found you."

Vladislav's impulsive tongue had backed them into a corner. Bogdan had no magic, no tricks which might fool even these most ignorant of men. His only option was to use their fear, and the inexplicable loss of so many of their men, against them. If he appeared weak they were as good as dead.

"It's done," he said, as though his spell had already been cast.

The scarred man laughed. "But what have you done, Bogdan the Great? My eyes have not lost sight of you, and I've seen nothing which might convince me."

"Just because you can't see it, doesn't mean it hasn't been done."

"If this a trick, you shall pay with your life."

Bogdan waved a hand toward the six dead bodies still spread beside him on the ground. "Why don't you ask your friends? You shall join them soon enough."

The man's face flushed with anger. "Tell me," he said. "Tell me what you have done."

"Can you feel it? Even now as we speak the curse is seeping into your bones. Soon it will take hold and there will be no stopping it. Before the moon is once again full in the sky, every last one of you will be dead."

"I feel it!" The toothless man cried out as if he was already suffering in agony. "I feel his loathsome curse in my bones!"

The cries of the toothless man were met by others, until a great panic had descended again over the campsite. But Bogdan would not rest. If he was to convince them beyond all doubt, he would need to drive them mad and shatter whatever was left of their spirits. And so it was his turn to laugh. He threw his head back to face the sky and laughed like a demon—a demon who had claimed another soul for Satan. When at last he stopped, he set his gaze upon the eyes of the scarred man.

They were eyes which shone bright with fear. "Is it too late? Can the curse be lifted?"

"Why should I do such a thing? You have tasted human flesh, and I have no doubt you'll taste it again."

"What would you ask of us?" The scarred man dropped to a knee and ran his fingers through his coarse, red hair.

"Swear an oath," said Bogdan. "You must never again raise human flesh to your lips."

"I swear," he said. "I swear before the earth and the sky and the Lord in Heaven, not a single man among us will eat the meat of another."

Bogdan closed his eyes and opened them softly for dramatic effect. "Then it's settled. But I must warn you that should you break your oath, and taste the flesh of men, it will turn to poison inside your stomach and you will rot from the inside out."

They came one at a time before him and kneeled, each repeating the same vow that had been made by their leader. When it was finished the horses were returned, and as promised, Bogdan and his companions were guided without incident to the place where they had been ambushed.

Svyatoslav was happy to find his pipe still stashed away in his saddle bag. "In all my years as a soldier, venturing far and wide through distant lands, I've never seen anything to match such horrors. Our mission is truly blessed, for only the Lord could deliver us from the jaws of cannibals."

"Yes," said Bogdan. "We are indeed blessed, but it was not the Lord who saved us. It was the very creature we seek to destroy."

The big man smiled as he packed his pipe. "God works through all things, my friend."

Maybe Svyatoslav was right, but Bogdan was tired and his head hurt, and they had many long hours of riding ahead of them. Whatever the evil spirit's intentions at the campsite had been, he thought it was still unwise for them to sleep through the night.

"Vladislav!" The big man rode up beside the boy and landed a hearty slap across his back. "You must never whistle again!"

TWENTY-ONE

Stale air burned in her lungs until she reminded herself to breath. Her body was stiff with anticipation. Word had finally come down from the judge. The jury had reached an unanimous verdict.

After a night of fitful sleep, she'd been escorted into the courtroom by Mr. Bennett's assistant, a young women who was only in her twenties, but who wore the studious face of someone much older.

"This way," said the assistant, her face framed by thick-rimmed glasses. She ushered Nancy into position just be-hind the defense table, where her husband was already seated alongside his attorney. "I've been holding a place for you."

"Thank you." She forced a thin smile across her lips and took a seat.

Byron turned and blew her a kiss as they stood for the judge's entrance.

They were expecting the worst. The new evidence had been damning. It wasn't hard for the prosecution to paint her husband as a sophisticated white collar criminal. One after another they detailed offshore accounts in the Cayman Islands, Bermuda, Panama, and Switzerland—each stuffed with a million dollars or more of money that had been siphoned off from investor accounts by a network of shell companies and trusts. There was even a bogus development company in a place called Georgia, a tiny country in the Caucuses, nestled between Turkey and Russia. The only Georgia Nancy had ever heard of was the state made famous for its peaches.

Still, Nancy held out hope for some miracle. In his closing statement, Mr. Bennett told a different story, choosing to focus on the Hardaway's active involvement in local charities, and the regular donations they'd made to the cancer center at Boston Children's Hospital.

She'd left that day feeling somewhat optimistic, but the two weeks of jury deliberations had taken a heavy toll on her spirits. The days at home had passed slowly, and she found herself wishing more than once for the dreadful monotony of the courtroom. She'd spent most days in bed, her only relief the assortment of pills she'd been prescribed by her psychiatrist. There was nothing worse, she thought more than once as the weeks dragged on, than frozen time.

Byron had fared no better. On the night she'd planned to share her revelations about the nanny, she found him babbling to himself in his study. It would have to wait, she'd told herself as she stood outside the study door listening to her husband babble, for a better time. But a better time had never come.

And so the fragile balance in the Hardaway home held steady, until the lawyer called to say the jury had reached a verdict. Now, as she faced the possibility of a life without her husband, without a father to raise their daughter, she would have given anything to go back to the beginning. She'd pushed him too hard. She'd wanted too much. She was as responsible for their destruction as he.

"Has the jury reached a verdict?" The old judge repeated the same formality she'd heard a hundred times on the legal procedurals she sometimes liked to watch.

The jury forewoman, a public school teacher who'd taken copious notes throughout the trial, took her position at the front of the jury box. "Yes, Your Honor, we have."

"Very well," said the judge. "Please inform the court of your decision."

The forewoman cleared her throat. "On the charge of bank fraud, we find the defendant guilty."

A cheer erupted from the gallery. The judge banged his gavel and called the room back to order. Nancy thought she was going to be sick.

"On the charge of embezzlement, we the members of the jury find the defendant guilty."

The onlookers, notable victims of her husband's crimes and their immediate family members, cheered again. This time, the judge sent officers out into the gallery and threatened to clear the courtroom.

Nancy's head spun as the forewoman continued. Tax evasion—guilty. The guilty verdicts kept coming, until her vision narrowed down to a single point and then everything went black.

The next thing she remembered was an officer holding a wet towel over her forehead, and the piercing flicker of fluorescent lights.

"Ma'am, you okay? Do you need an ambulance?"

"No." She struggled to get back up to her feet. "No ambulance. Where's my husband?"

"Take it easy, Mrs. Hardaway. You took a pretty good knock to the head when you blacked out."

She was in a strange room, with only the officer for company. "My husband—where's Byron? Where have they taken him?"

Mr. Bennett appeared in the doorway. "Nancy, I've been looking everywhere for you. Are you okay?"

"Yes, Anthony. I'm fine." She hated being treated like a delicate flower. Men were always doing that. "Will somebody please tell me where Byron is?"

"He's in custody," said the lawyer. "I asked the judge to extend bail until the sentencing hearing, but my request was denied."

She thought she might collapse again and fought hard to stay on her feet. As much as she'd prepared herself for the day she might finally lose him, imagining it over and over in those idle moments in the courtroom, it came like a rush of blood to the head. It was over, she thought, and there was nothing more to be done. She wondered how long he would be gone.

"The car's waiting," said Mr. Bennett. "Please, let me at least see you home."

"Are they out there?"

"Who?"

"The reporters. Those lecherous parasites can't wait to get their money shot for the evening news—the fallen socialite." She would have watched the same thing herself had she not been cast in the starring role.

"Hold your head up, Nancy. No need for shame. You're a victim of this as much as anyone."

She cast a sideways look at the officer before returning her eyes to the lawyer. "Anthony, we both know that's not true. I pushed him. I wanted more and more, and if he hadn't been caught it would have never stopped." Tears welled up in her eyes and spilled over, running in thin lines down her cheeks.

Mr. Bennett removed the fancy handkerchief from his breast pocket, the kind that was normally only for show, and dabbed her tears away. "Come on," he said. "Let's get you cleaned up. I won't have you looking like the star of a Lifetime movie."

She did as the lawyer had said, and held her head high as they passed the sea of reporters gathered outside on the steps of the courthouse. Microphones were shoved in her face. Camera lenses framed her from all directions. But not once did she waver. Not once did she give them the satisfaction of recording her tears.

As the car pulled away, she turned her attention back to practical matters. "What happens next? Will he go straight to prison?"

Mr. Bennett, who had seemed more flustered by the media than she, straightened his tie and smoothed his jacket. "No, now we wait for sentencing. The judge set a date in two months."

"Two months?"

"It's typical," he said. "He needs time to review the details of the case before deciding on an appropriate sentence. In the meantime, I'll make another petition to extend bail until the hearing. It's certainly not unheard of in white collar cases."

"So he might come home?"

"At least until the sentencing. But don't get your hopes up, Nancy. I'm a good lawyer, some might say a great lawyer, but the decision rests with the judge."

If you're such a great lawyer, she thought, Byron would be riding home with us. "And what happens after sentencing? Then will he go to prison?"

The lawyer straightened his tie again. "It's hard to say. In the past, he might have gotten away with some probation, maybe a term of house arrest. But the public sentiment has shifted, and the courts have responded with tougher sentencing guidelines."

"How long?"

"Nancy—"

"How long, Anthony?"

"If I had to guess, and mind you this is only a rough estimate, I'd say Byron is looking at five to ten years in federal prison. With good behavior, he could be out in as little as two or three."

Five to ten years. It was a long time. Nora would be in elementary school. Nancy wondered if their daughter would even recognize Byron when he came home, the father who'd spent her childhood in federal prison.

Did it even matter? She was hardly a present mother. Nora's first word had not been 'mommy,' but the name of the old nanny. Was it too late for them to be good parents? Was it too late to give their only daughter the attention and love she deserved?

As the car approached the house, she was relieved to see the street was empty. The media already had their fill of soundbites, their videoclips for the six o'clock news. Soon, there would be another drama to fill the space between advertisements for smartphones and the latest blood pressure medications. They'd move on as quickly as they'd come, and the Hardaways would be forgotten.

Her attention drifted to the sights of the city passing by outside the window. Boston had been home all her life. But now, with her husband on his way to prison, and the life they'd made shattered to pieces, it was less like home and more like some foreign, distant place she could no longer recognize. She closed her eyes and opened them again, hoping for a moment it was only a bad dream.

"There's one more thing, Nancy."

Her attention snapped back to the confines of the hired sedan. "Can it wait?"

The lawyer sucked in air through the corners of his mouth. "It's best to get ahead of these things. I don't want you to be caught unprepared."

"Unprepared for what?"

"It's normal practice in these cases for the judge to order restitution."

"Restitution?"

"Yes, the court will seize your assets, and sell them off to pay the victims back for their losses."

"What about Nora's trust?" Her daughter's trust was the only thing keeping them going month-to-month since the start of her husband's trial.

"It's hard to say. But nothing is sacred, not in the eyes of the court. If you have any precious family heirlooms, jewelry that belonged to a grandmother or a great aunt, I'd find a box and bury it."

"And the house?"

"It won't be long."

So this is how it ends, she thought, a disgraced mother and her helpless daughter, wandering together through the cold streets of Boston. She imagined herself begging for change. "Can't you do something?"

"Look," he said, "they won't exactly throw you out on the street, not with a baby girl. I expect they'll allow you enough to rent a small apartment, maybe a second-hand car to get yourself around."

Nancy's worst fear had come true. She would have to be normal, to live like those woman she saw stuffing their snot-nosed kids into the backs of minivans and buying in bulk at the local Costco.

She would have rather died in the streets.

She took great care closing the heavy door behind her as she tiptoed into Byron's study. Inez would surely be listening for her return with keen ears, and although Nancy loved the woman, perhaps even more than she had loved her own mother, she couldn't bear the thought of facing her. It was only a matter of time before she would have to let her go.

Byron kept his most expensive bottles on the bottom shelf of the liquor cabinet. It was one of his stupid jokes, she thought, as she poured herself a glass of his single malt whiskey. Things wouldn't be the same without him. Her only hope now was that she might keep the house long enough to celebrate Nora's first birthday.

She took a sip of the whiskey and surveyed the room. It was all the same—the smell of the leather sofa, the unread books lining the shelves, and the desk where her husband had spent many long hours plotting the crimes that had brought their family to ruin. But something was different. Byron had been there only a few hours before, talking on the phone with Mr. Bennett as he prepared himself for the jury's verdict. But now he was gone and she was alone. She was unprepared for how much it hurt. A single tear rolled down her cheek.

No, she thought, I've done enough crying for the day. I have to be strong—strong enough to salvage whatever is left of Nora's future.

Another tear fell, then another. Maybe it was just the whiskey, or a general sense of exhaustion, or the empty relics of her husband. Maybe the years of expensive makeup and fake smiles and pretending to be happy had all finally converged on a single point. Whatever the cause might have been, the hard face she'd always worn—the same hard face that had once belonged to her mother—cracked into a thousand pieces. And she cried. She cried harder than she had ever cried before.

She thought she might cry forever, balled up on the sofa in a soggy mess of tears, but her sobs were interrupted by a knock on the study door.

"Please," she said. "Go away."

The door slid open to reveal the old nanny, shadows falling across the lines of her wrinkled face.

"What do you want?" She was surprised by the harsh tone of her own voice.

Iryna only smiled as she crossed the room and lowered herself to the sofa. "I had a husband once, same as you. Of course, I was much prettier back then, some might have said the prettiest girl in our village. Oh, you should have seen him—so handsome and funny."

It had never occurred to Nancy that the old nanny might have a story to tell—a life before the night she arrived on their doorstep. "What happened?"

"It was a beautiful spring day, and when he left with the other men to fish the North Atlantic, nobody could have imagined such a ferocious storm might appear in the skies above the sea." Iryna's gaze drifted off, as though she was reliving the tragedy in her mind. "A few pieces of their boat washed up on the beach in the weeks after, but the men were never found."

"I'm sorry."

"There's no need to be sorry, dear. It's only a distant memory, and they say time heals all wounds. My only regret was not having a child to call my own."

"Is that why you became a nanny?"

A light shone in the old woman's eyes. "I had so much love to give. It would be a shame if it went to waste."

"Iryna?"

"Yes, dear?"

"I'm a terrible mother." The thought had come to her before, in those rare moments in between pills when she'd had the clarity to be honest with herself, but it was the first time she'd ever said it aloud.

Iryna moved a hand to Nancy's knee. "You've been under a lot of stress. Don't judge yourself too harshly."

"It's true," she said. "Nora hardly recognizes me. It was your name she spoke first, not mine."

The nanny's face froze as though Nancy had caught her off guard. After a long pause, she lowered her shoulders and sighed. "I should have said something. It was anything but intentional, I promise."

Tears returned to Nancy's eyes—wet, salty rivers running down her face. "It's all my fault. I could have been there, but I was too busy attending parties and wooing clients for my husband. Now he's going to prison."

Iryna slid closer and wrapped her arms around Nancy's shoulders, pulled her tight to her chest. "That's it, dear. Let it come. Don't hold back."

She buried her face above the old woman's breast and cried one tear after another, until there were no more tears to cry. It felt good, being held as though she was only a child. Whatever lingering suspicions she still had about the discrepancies on Iryna's résumé were replaced by the woman's gentle compassion and love. Her mother had never held her that way, not even the time they came to say her grandmother had died.

"Come now," said the nanny. "I'll make some tea and draw a hot bath."

Nancy smiled. She wondered if tea and hot baths were Iryna's answer to everything.

She sent Inez home early. Still, the housekeeper had insisted on preparing dinner before she left.

"I won't have you going hungry," she'd said, as she fussed around in the kitchen.

Nancy tried to tell her the truth—in a matter of weeks she would be unable to pay her salary. But she couldn't bring herself to say anything. The thought of losing both her husband and her closest friend on the same day was too much for her to bear.

She sat at the kitchen table and poked at Inez's famous crab cakes. Baby Nora's cries had sent the nanny upstairs to the nursery. Alone and without appetite, Nancy pushed the plate aside and trudged up the stairs to the bedroom she'd once shared with her husband. Though she was tired—an exhaustion rooted deep down in her bones—her troubled thoughts prevented sleep.

She stared up at the coffered ceiling, replaying the events of the day in her mind, as she waited for the sleeping pill and a double dose of her precious anxiety medication to take full effect.

She had no memory of falling asleep, but not long after she'd drifted off, she awoke to find herself alone in a forest. It was night, and strange, twisted shadows fell at her feet. She ran, branches scratching at her face, until she reached the shore of a lake. Something behind her made a sound, and when she spun around she saw a pair of red eyes moving toward her in the dark.

She should have been afraid, but instead she welcomed him. It was a dance they'd done before—Nancy playing the part of the prey and he the hunter. She surrendered herself to him, and he took her her into his cold embrace.

Pleasure pulsed throughout her body. It was something sex with her husband had never been, a wordless energy that surged up from the base of her spine, crackling and tingling her skin like lightning in a storm.

She couldn't say how long it lasted. It could have been hours or only minutes. But when it was over, and she'd finally succumbed to the climax of her pleasure, he held her close as she drifted off once more into a deep, dreamless sleep.

She was jostled awake by the piercing wail of a siren and the screech of tires coming to a sudden stop in the driveway. Bouncing red and blue lights poured in through the window and filled the dark space of the master bedroom.

It was the police, she thought. They must have discovered her unsuccessful attempt to destroy the evidence of their offshore accounts. Or maybe Byron had finally cracked and said something he shouldn't have. They were coming to take her away, leaving Nora to fend for herself with neither a mother nor father. The poor girl would end up in one of those low-rent foster homes with six brothers and a mother with bad taste.

Nancy flung open the closet and wriggled into a pair of black jeans, threw on her favorite sweater. She wouldn't have them taking her to jail in her nightgown. Her face had already been all over the news, but a mugshot was something else entirely.

She fumbled for her phone in the dark, not daring to turn on the lights and make herself an easy catch. She hoped she had time for one last phone call to the lawyer before they led her away in handcuffs. Mr. Bennett had, of course, given her his personal cell phone number, and she dialed it as she edged toward the window.

"Yes?" The voice on the other end was slow and scratchy, as if the lawyer had also been asleep.

"It's Nancy," she said. "I don't have much time. The police have come for me."

"What are you talking about, Nancy?"

She peered out the window at the source of the red and blue lights. It wasn't a police car as she had expected, but an ambulance. "Just a second, Anthony."

"What the hell is going on over there?"

Down below, two paramedics in white shirts jogged past the front door toward the entrance to the basement apartment. The caretaker was waving his arms in a panic.

"False alarm," she said. "I'll have to call you back."

She hung up before the over-priced lawyer could ask more questions—the only thing lawyers ever did was ask questions—and made her way out to the sidewalk. The ambulance had been joined by a police car, and for a moment she thought it was all just a ploy to lure her out. It was only when she heard the panic-stricken cries of the caretaker that she knew something terrible had happened.

"My son!" Tears gushed down the man's face. "Please God, help my son!"

"What's happened, Leroy?"

"It's Connor. He's not moving, Nancy. And when I touched him he was cold."

A police officer stepped in between them. "Are you the boy's mother?"

"No, but it's my house." It was still true, at least for a little while longer.

"You'll have to move aside." The police officer motioned her back and turned his attention to the boy's father, who'd collapsed to the ground in a puddle of tears.

She could only watch the horrific spectacle unfold—the arrival of more police vehicles, the paramedics breaking the dreadful news to a devastated father, and the team from the medical examiner's office removing the boy's body on a wheeled gurney. It was gruesome, seeing a young life with its myriad possibilities reduced to nothing more than a black plastic bodybag.

Iryna emerged from the house with hot tea. Nancy was still on the sidewalk, sweater pulled tight against the cool night air. It hadn't occurred to her to check on her own slumbering daughter until she caught sight of the nanny. "How's the baby?"

"She's fine, dear. Sleeping like an angel."

Just then something caught her attention. Maybe it was only the rustle of leaves in the wind, but Nancy thought she heard someone whisper her name. "Did you hear that?"

"Hear what?" The old woman cocked her head to the side and raised a single eyebrow.

"Oh, it's nothing," she said. But as she gazed out into a darkened corner across the street, she saw a pair of red, glowing eyes staring back at her through the night.

TWENTY-TWO

"Have you ever seen anything like it?" Vladislav's young eyes were as wide as saucers.

"No," said Bogdan. In fact, it was unlike anything he could have imagined. The city sprawled out before them in a tangled web, red tiled roofs extending in all directions. At the center of it all, the green, slow-moving waters of a wide river cut the city into two equal halves, joined together by the symmetrical stone arches of a half dozen bridges.

Svyatoslav shrugged it off. He was the only one among them who, before their arduous journey over the mountains, had ever traveled more than a day or two from their village. "If you think that's impressive, you should see Kyiv."

Bogdan didn't care what Svyatoslav thought. They'd only just descended the last mountain pass when they first caught sight of the city. It was enough to take his breath away, but he couldn't help wondering where in all that tangled mess they might begin.

"Let's find a tavern," said the big man.

"A tavern?"

Svyatoslav slapped his forehead. "A tavern is where people gather to drink. I'm in need of some libations, and we can take a room to rest up. I'm tired of sleeping on sticks and stones."

Vladislav's face lit up. "I need a drink, too."

"No," said Svyatoslav. "What you need, my young friend, is a proper bath. You stink."

The boy raised an arm and sniffed. A joke had passed among them, in those tired moments when they'd stopped to bed down for the day, that not even the evil spirit would dare approach them once Vladislav had taken off his boots.

"But we don't have any money." Bogdan felt ill prepared for the demands of the city. What did a handful of poor peasants know about such things?

Svyatoslav rode up beside him and slapped him across the back. "Come now, you didn't really think I planned to continue camping in the woods and chewing on dried meat? Stick with your old friend. I'll take care of everything."

They rode together through the outskirts of the city, passing several taverns until the big man declared one suitable for his purposes. Once inside, he shuffled up to a game of dice that was already in progress. With great ceremony, he placed his wedding ring on the table.

The rules of the game were as foreign to Bogdan as the language the men spoke. Svyatoslav appeared unbothered, communicating in grunts and whoops and a great variety of hand gestures. It was fun, watching the big man roll the dice, though Bogdan couldn't be sure who was winning and who was losing. It wasn't until Svyatoslav passed a coin to a girl in a smock, who returned some minutes later with two wooden cups filled with beer, that he knew fortune was in their favor.

The beer was sour, but it felt good passing between his cracked and broken lips. It had been a month since they'd left the village. The journey through the mountains had taken a heavy toll on their tired bodies, and it would be in their best interests, he thought, to recover some of their strength before searching for the source of the evil spirit.

In another hour, Svyatoslav had earned enough coins to send Vladislav upstairs with one of the tavern maids, a pretty girl who spoke a few words of their language.

"Mind your hands," he said. "I've only paid for the hot bath."

Bogdan sipped his beer and canvassed the tavern's common room. It was a dingy place, perfect for a seedy game of dice, with low-hanging rafters that sagged beneath the weight of the floors above. Young girls in smocks moved from table to table, dodging the wandering hands of ragged men whose wives, he imagined, might be relieved they were not at home.

Svyatoslav carried on well into the night. Several hours had passed when he finally gave up the dice and joined Bogdan. "My friend," he said, tossing a bag heavy with coins on the rough planks of the table, "we've enough there for a warm meal and a soft bed."

"You've been lucky, though was it wise to gamble your wedding ring?"

The big man snorted. "It's not gambling when you know you're going to win."

Once again, Bogdan found himself glad for the able company of his friend. "Where'd you learn to play dice like that?"

"When I was a young man, not much older than you are now, I joined a company of soldiers on an expedition to a place called Prussia, far to the north." He signaled one of the tavern maids for another beer. "It was a long and brutal winter. Many perished in the snow, but my unit took shelter in an old barn. There was nothing to do for months but shiver and roll the dice. By the time spring finally arrived I was a rich man."

"But why did you leave the village? The life of a soldier is hardly easy."

The maid returned with the beer. Svyatoslav took a long sip before dabbing the brown liquid from his beard with the sleeve of his shirt. "I was a restless young man," he said. "Restless and very angry."

It was difficult for Bogdan to imagine his friend as anything but the patient and humorous man he had always known. "Angry?"

Svyatoslav took another sip of his beer. "Two years before I left, it fell on my family to make the sacrifice. I watched as they cut my brother down from the tree and burned his body on the pyre."

Bogdan was surprised by the revelation. "I'm sorry," he said. "I didn't know."

The big man waved it off. "I've long since made peace with it, but not before sending many young and ambitious men to an early death with the blade of my axe. My only wish now is that God might forgive me."

This time it was Bogdan who signaled for another beer. He remembered the night he'd sacrificed himself for the second time. It was Svyatoslav who'd insisted on tying him to the tree. "It must have been hard, sending me to die with the memory of your brother still lingering in the past."

"You're wrong," he said. "I wasn't sending you to your death. I knew you would live."

"How?"

"Because you didn't die the first time."

What his friend had said made sense. Even Bogdan, willing as he'd been to give his life to save the village, had expected he might survive his second brush with the evil spirit. "But could you be sure?"

Svyatoslav drew his eyebrows together as he loaded more of his precious dried herbs into his pipe. "How can anyone be sure of anything? These are strange times, and there is more to the world than we might ever hope to understand.

"But one thing is certain. Hundreds of boys were tied to that tree, and hundreds of boys met their end. I knew, from the very moment we cut you down, that my fate, and the fate of our village, was wrapped up with yours. I would follow you to the Gates of Hell and beyond, Bogdan the Great. I would follow you with a smile on my ugly old face."

Bogdan was considering the words of his wise old friend when a commotion at the far end of the tavern grabbed his attention.

It was Vladislav, naked as the day he was born, tearing down the stairs with his clothes in one hand and his boots in the other. A fat man with a large knife chased after him, shouting words Bogdan couldn't understand.

Vladislav wasn't taking any chances with the knife. He leapt from the staircase before reaching the bottom, crashing into a table and sending cups of beer flying in all directions. Bogdan thought he might be hurt, but the boy leapt to his bare feet and scurried out the tavern door as a chorus of boos and cheers erupted.

"I told him to mind his hands," said Svyatoslav, as he started for the door. "I'll kill him myself if the tavern keeper doesn't get to him first."

They found him around the corner, bent over against a wall and catching his breath after his hasty flight down the stairs. He stood up when he saw them approaching, and raised his hands in front of him in a gesture of innocence— the same gesture all those who are guilty make—as if to say he'd done nothing wrong.

Svyatoslav took him by the upper arm, his meaty fingers burying themselves into the skinny boy's wiry muscles. "What did you do?"

"Let go," he said. He tried pulling his arm away, but Svyatoslav's firm grip was too much for him. "She said it was on the house—said she took a liking to me."

Bogdan had no idea what Vladislav was talking about, though he guessed it might have something to do with the pretty girl who'd taken him upstairs for a bath.

"They always say that." Svyatoslav was still jerking the boy around by his arm. "First they bed you, and then they demand your money. I've seen it a hundred times. You're lucky that fat man with the knife didn't slice your little pecker off."

Vladislav made an unsuccessful attempt to cover himself with his free hand, as if he'd only just become aware of his nakedness. "That's not fair!"

"That's the city," said the big man. He released his grip on the boy's arm and raised an eyebrow. "Was it your first time?"

Vladislav grinned from ear to ear, then dropped to the ground and fumbled around for his clothes.

They had just untied the horses, intent on finding another place in which to rest up, when a strange voice called out from behind. "Hello," it said. "Hello, my friends. Hello."

Bogdan turned to see a man shuffling toward them from the direction of the tavern. He thought it might have been the tavern keeper, but as the man grew closer he recognized him from one of the tables near where he and Svyatoslav had been drinking beer.

"Hello," the man said again. He spoke in their language, but with an accent unlike their own. "I mean you no harm."

Svyatoslav spoke first. "What do you want?"

"I wouldn't normally follow you out into the night, but it's clear you're not from these parts and you might require some kind of assistance." He held out his hands, palms open —a symbol of peace. "My name is Ion."

"That's very kind," said the big man. "But we don't need any help."

"Oh, really?"

There was something curious about the man's voice. Bogdan couldn't be sure whether it was just his accent, or if some sinister thought swirled behind those eyes—black as coal. "Why have you followed us? The last man who followed us is dead."

"Please, forgive me." Ion brought his open hands together as if to plead for mercy. "My mother always said it was rude to eavesdrop on other people's conversations, but I couldn't help hearing something about an evil spirit. It's been a long time since I've heard such things."

Bogdan looked around, unsure of what to say next or whether he could trust him. But if Ion knew something about the evil spirit, he wanted to find out. It was, after all, why they'd come to the city. He decided it would be necessary to take the risk. "Do your people make the sacrifice?"

Svyatoslav tried to stop him, but it was too late. The words had already come.

"Sacrifice?" Ion rubbed his chin and fixed his black eyes on a single point somewhere in the distance. "I thought that was only a myth. I've heard the stories, of course, on my trade runs up north, but I never imagined they might be true."

Vladislav had tugged his pants on and was working on his boots. "It's true! Bogdan—"

Svyatoslav gripped the boy's arm again to silence him. "Quiet," he said. "We're in the company of strangers."

"Strangers—yes," said Ion. "That's something we shall have to remedy over a round of beer. I know a place not far from here."

Bogdan looked to Svyatoslav the way a child might look to a parent for permission. The big man shrugged his wide shoulders. "Why not? We're in need of another tavern."

"And this happens every year—a new boy is sent to die?" Ion wiped beer from his thick lips. He'd brought them to another tavern, this place even more cramped and dirty than the first. They'd found a suitable table in the corner, and Bogdan told him the story of their village and the sacrifice and the spirit who wouldn't rest until he'd had his revenge.

"Yes," he said. "It happens every year, at least it did until I broke the tradition. But what of the city? Are you not haunted by the spirit of the evil prince?"

"Vlad," said Ion. "You mean Vlad Ţepeş—they called him Vlad the Impaler, and come morning, you'll see his ruinous old castle on the hill." A tavern maid sided up to the table with five sloppy mugs of beer, and Ion waited until she was clear before continuing. "His thirst for blood was the stuff of legends. The old folks tell a story not unlike your own, that exactly one month after he was hanged from the castle walls, the people of this city began to die mysterious deaths. Young folks, strong and healthy, went to bed and never woke up. But that was a long time ago. No one gives much thought to Vlad these days."

"What changed?" Bogdan had little doubt about the story. But if what Ion said was true—the spirit of the evil prince no longer troubled them—perhaps there was a way to lift the curse upon his village.

"They dug him up," said Ion, "and drove a silver stake into his heart."

"And it worked?"

Ion nodded. "So they say. If I might speak plainly, the only evil in this city is the greed and treachery of its living, breathing residents. Of course, there are those in the villages, peasants with their superstitions and old wives' tales, who still speak of strigoi and the dead who come out at night to wander."

"Strigoi?"

The man with the black eyes smiled. "I believe the word in your language is vampire—only instead of drinking blood they steal your soul."

It was the last words he said that gave Bogdan pause to think. He wondered if the souls of those who had died in his village had made their way to heaven.

Svyatoslav's son, who had remained so silent since their arrival in the city that Bogdan almost forgot his presence, cleared his throat and spoke. "There's only one thing that doesn't make sense. If it's as you say, and the evil prince was finally sent to Hell with a silver stake in his heart, then why does he continue to plague our poor village?"

"Ah, the silent one has spoken." Ion waved an index finger in the air. "My friend, I'm afraid I don't have the answer to your question. But perhaps I might be able to help in some small way."

"How?" While Ion's story had given them a name—Vlad Țepeș, the one they called the Impaler—Bogdan was beginning to suspect their grueling journey to the city was nothing more than a dead end. He tried not to think too much about the long trip back home, and the disappointment that might await him there.

"Perhaps," said the man with black eyes, "you'd like to see the evil prince for yourself."

I have seen him, he thought, many times. Those red eyes were not so easy to forget. "What do you mean?"

Ion finished the last of his beer and placed the empty mug on the table. "I haven't told you how the story ends. It's difficult to imagine, really, but when they dug up our old friend Vlad, he was as fresh as the day he died, minus the head, which they'd mounted on a pike until his skull was picked clean by the birds. Some say his heart was still beating in his chest, that is, until they drove the stake through it. But these details are insignificant. What matters is what they did next, for the body was not returned to its original grave. They carried him, under cover of darkness and sworn to secrecy, to an unmarked grave far beyond the city gates. It's there he remains to this day."

"I don't suppose you know the location of this unmarked grave."

Ion's face twisted into a wide, toothy grin. "It's the worst kept secret in the city."

Maybe it was only the dank, dark space of the tavern, or the way the deep lines of the man's face filled with shadow, but something about Ion's smile said he was enjoying himself. Bogdan wondered if it was all a game, just another story he would tell his friends about the dimwitted peasants from up north. Still, what choice did he have but to trust the man? "You say it's far beyond the gates. How far?"

"On horseback? Maybe one hour. If you'd like I can take you there—give myself a good reason to escape the cramped confines of the city—and still make it back in time for dinner." He grinned again. "My wife makes the best sarmale this side of the river."

Bogdan was about to reply when Svyatoslav interrupted. "And how much will your expert assistance cost us?"

Ion's grin shifted into a frown. "My friend, I'm hurt by your presumption. I know how hard it can be to find your way in a strange and unfamiliar land. I ask not for money, but for a few stories and laughs shared among good company. It would seem your village is in dire need of a helping hand, and I offer mine freely."

"When?" Bogdan's skin tingled as he imagined himself standing above the evil spirit's grave. "When can you take us?"

Ion took his time, as though he was considering practical matters. "I have some business to attend to tomorrow—a new shipment of goods up from Bucharest. How about the day after?"

Two days. He'd come this far, he could wait another two days. "Perfect."

"I don't like it," said Svyatoslav. It was the fifth time he'd said as much since Bogdan had first accepted Ion's offer. "I don't like it, but I'll go along with it. Somebody has to keep you safe."

Bogdan had grown accustomed to his regular protests. The big man was careful, never one for unnecessary risk. It was a trait that had served him well in his many years of fighting in foreign wars.

They'd passed the day sleeping in a rented room above the tavern. There was only one bed, which Svyatoslav had insisted Bogdan share with young Vladislav. He and his son would be fine, he'd said, on the floor. But the comforts of a bed had done Bogdan little good. He'd spent most of the day awake, fractured thoughts spinning through his head, as Vladislav slept snuggled up peacefully beside him. He felt something like relief when the sky beyond the window finally darkened and his friends stirred themselves back to life. Only Vladislav required extra nudging.

"Let's be smart about this," said Svyatoslav, as they prepared to head back down to the common room in search of dinner. "I won't have us walking into some kind of trap."

Bogdan wanted to tell him he was being silly. Ion was just an old merchant trader, probably bored and eager for a day away from his wife. But he'd seen enough in the last year to convince him anything was possible. "What would you suggest?"

"Any general worth his weight in salt knows you should never leave yourself with a single option. Things can change quickly in the heat of battle. If we were an army, and I was the general, I'd want the element of surprise."

Bogdan didn't know anything about armies. The only thing he knew in that moment was the hunger growing in his belly. "How do we surprise someone who knows we're coming?"

"We split up," said the big man. "My son can follow behind and remain out of sight. If all goes well we won't have need of him. But if it's a trap, or things go bad, we'll be glad he has our backs."

"Very well."

"One last thing—the boy stays here in the room. I'll pay for another night."

"No!" Vladislav had been preoccupied with lacing up his boots, but at the mention of his name he jumped to his feet. "Please, Bogdan! You can't make me stay."

"It's only right," said the big man. "You're too young, and someone has to watch our things."

"Was I too young to be eaten by wild cannibals? If I hadn't fed them a line about Bogdan's magic, we might all be dead."

"It was quick thinking," said Bogdan. "You've proven your worth. But Svyatoslav is right. Someone needs to stay put and watch our things."

He'd expected Vladislav to argue, but the boy dropped his gaze down to his untied boots. "If that's what you want, then that's what I'll do."

Just maybe, thought Bogdan, Vladislav is learning what it means to be a man.

They passed most of the night in the common room, Svyatoslav racking up more coins at the dice table and Vladislav sulking with a beer. The tavern—which had been busy well past midnight—was nearly empty when dawn finally broke.

The plan was simple. Bogdan and Svyatoslav would ride out to the place where Ion had promised to meet them. Svyatoslav's son would follow well behind on foot. Vladislav had only to stay out of trouble, and was forbidden from socializing with tavern maids. "Flash them so much as a smile," Svyatoslav had said, "and I'll cut off your pecker myself."

And so the mood was generally light when they rode off as a pair, hopeful but unsure of what fortunes the day might bring.

The man with black eyes was, as promised, waiting for their arrival atop a horse which, by its haggard appearance, had seen better days. "Hello, my friends. Only two? Where are the others?"

Bogdan thought he saw a hint of disappointment on the man's face. "I'm afraid they've had too much to drink. The beer is much better than anything we have back home."

Whatever disappointment Ion had shown was erased by a smile. "Yes," he said. "Our city is famous for the quality of its beer. It's the water—snowmelt from the mountains."

In short time, the city gave way to the forest. The horses grunted and flared their nostrils, heavy breaths visible in the chilly morning air, as they followed a steep track up into the foothills.

Bogdan was happy to leave the city behind. It had only been two days, and already he felt like a chicken in a cage. While he hoped to find some answer that might lift the curse, he was eager to get back to the village—eager to hold his son. Still, there was some fear about what awaited his return. More than once, in those fleeting moments of fitful sleep, he'd dreamed they were all dead, every last soul in the village consumed by the evil spirit of Vlad the Impaler.

They'd just crested the first of the foothills, mountains rising up in the distance, when Ion turned around in his saddle. "Won't be long now."

Halfway down there was a small clearing, a place where the hill leveled off and the trees opened to a view of the river below—white water cascading over boulders as it began its final descent toward the city.

"Here," said Ion, pointing to a spot on the ground. "I give you the final resting place of Vlad Țepeș."

Bogdan climbed down from his horse and looked around. Other than the impressive view, the location was entirely unremarkable. There was no cross, no headstone, nothing to mark the grave of a fearsome and bloodthirsty man who had once carved out an expansive principality with his iron fist.

Svyatoslav shrugged. "What now?"

"I don't know." Bogdan stood above the spot where Ion had pointed.

"Do you feel anything?"

He closed his eyes and listened, hoping for a sign, something to signal the presence of the evil spirit. The only sounds were the gentle stirrings of the forest and the rushing waters of the river below. "No," he said. "I don't feel anything."

Svyatoslav dismounted and joined him. They waited together for something, anything, that might lead them toward the answer they were so desperately seeking.

"I'm sorry to disappoint you." Ion hadn't bothered to climb down from his horse. "He's been dead a very long time, you know."

Bogdan was still listening, his eyes closed tightly against the mid-morning sun, when he heard the sound of horses approaching from the forest.

Svyatoslav must have heard them too. "Listen," he said. "Do you hear that?"

Three more riders emerged from the trees and took up position next to Ion. The largest among them was armed with a heavy axe, much like the one Svyatoslav had left back at the tavern.

"What's this?" Bogdan said.

"I warned you," said the man with black eyes, as that same toothy grin spread over his face. "The only evil in our city is the treachery of its residents."

Svyatoslav had been right. It was trap, and they'd been lead willingly like cows to the slaughter. Bogdan's heart stirred in his chest, blood rising up and beating in his ears. "What do you want?"

"Easy now," said Ion. "Nobody has to die. We only want the horses, and whatever else you might be carrying." He pointed in Svyatoslav's direction. "I've had my eye on that gold ring since you first put it down on a game of dice. Is it real?"

"Real enough," said the big man. "But I have no intention of letting it go."

Ion scoffed. "My friends have come all the way out here on the promise of four horses. I'll need something to make it up to them."

Bogdan wondered if they should run, make a break for the horses and disappear into the forest. But they were unarmed and in unfamiliar territory. If they could only hold them off until nightfall, perhaps the evil spirit of Vlad Țepeș would come to claim them, as he'd claimed the cannibal king.

The opportunity came when the man with the axe said something to Ion in their language. The words were too foreign for Bogdan to understand, but it mattered little. They began to squabble among themselves, and Bogdan saw his chance.

He never had to take it.

An arrow hissed past his shoulder and stung its target. The man with the axe fell from his horse, screaming and writhing in agony. Svyatoslav moved quickly, much faster than any man his age should move, wresting the heavy axe from the fallen man's grip and burying it into his skull with a single blow.

A second arrow flew from the trees and found flesh. This time it was Ion who fell from his horse. Svyatoslav was on him just as quickly as he'd moved on the first, raising the axe above his head in a high arc and bringing it down in a violent blow that sent the man's head rolling away from his shoulders. It came to rest at Bogdan's feet, black eyes staring up at him with an expression that might have been disbelief.

Bogdan had seen many things in his short life, but he had never seen the horrors of battle. He could only watch, frozen and bewildered, as the two other men who had come to rob them kicked their horses and galloped away. It was over as quickly as it had begun.

"Are you okay?" It was Svyatoslav, who'd placed a blood-stained hand on his shoulder.

"Yes," he said, though in truth his vision had gone blurry and the world spun. He dropped to one knee and steadied himself.

"Sit," said his friend. "It's normal. A few more deep breaths and it'll pass."

For a moment, he thought he saw Yekaterina appear from the forest, but as his vision cleared he recognized a familiar face—Svyatoslav's son.

The two men, father and son, embraced and exchanged subtle nods without speaking a single word.

And so it was Bogdan, feeling somewhat recovered, who spoke first. "Will they return?"

"Alone?" said the big man. "Not a chance. Though I suggest we don't linger any longer than necessary. It's possible they went to fetch more friends."

Bogan couldn't help feeling disappointed. They were no closer to saving their village than when they'd left. He waved a hand toward the two bodies spread lifeless in the dirt, one with a crushed skull and the other without a head. "What should we do with them?"

Svyatoslav smiled. "We bury them." His old, smoke-stained teeth appeared white against his blood-splattered face. "I know just the place to dig a hole."

They'd dug many holes together, though this was the first without the benefit of a proper shovel. They took turns, the big man breaking up the dirt with the blade of his new axe, only stopping to rest as the two younger men scraped at the softened earth with bare hands.

It was slow going, and the sun was high in the sky when the axe struck wood. It took another hour to clear the rest of the dirt away, revealing the lid of a long wooden box that resembled something like a coffin.

Bogdan ran his fingers over the spongy, badly decomposed wood. A slight tingle ran up his arm. He couldn't be sure if it was the same feeling he'd had on more than one occasion when the evil spirit had been near, or if it was nothing more than anticipation for whatever they might find hidden away inside.

"Are you ready?" Svyatoslav hoisted the axe above his head for the final blow.

He nodded.

The big man swung and the axe fell, pieces of wood col-
lapsing into the dark, hollow space within the box. They
dropped to their knees, pulled the rotting planks free until
the contents were exposed to the light of day.

If Bogdan had expected to find the prince, well-pre-
served and intact save for a missing head, he would have
faced more disappointment. Whatever the evil prince had
once been was no longer—the ravages of time had reduced
his former glory to a pile of dust.

"Is it him?" Svyatoslav wiped blood from his hands and
lit his pipe with a flint-stone. "Could just be another one of
Ion's lies."

Bogdan scanned the forest, hoping for a glimpse of the
evil spirit, or something that would confirm the ashen
corpse in the grave was his. He closed his eyes again and
waited, as he'd done in the moments before Ion's treachery.
But there was nothing, only the steady hum of the river and
the chirping of birds.

Then it came to him—one last hope in his search for
some kind of answer.

He lowered himself closer to the wooden box and ran a
hand through bits of dust and bone. He'd almost given up
when he felt something cold and hard. "Hold on," he said.
"I think I've found something."

He wiped the dust off with his shirt and held it above
his head, glistening and shiny in the sun. It was a metal
stake, sharpened to a fine point at one end, and though
Bogdan knew little of precious metals, he knew without a
doubt it was made of silver.

TWENTY-THREE

"Please stay!" Nancy followed the housekeeper toward the front door with a cup of tea in her hand. Hot liquid spilled and splashed on the hardwood floor. Normally, she would have loathed such a mess, but as the days dragged on, she found herself giving less consideration to the things that had once mattered so much to her.

Inez had returned only long enough to gather her things. "I'm sorry, Nancy. But that poor boy's death was the last straw. Something about this old house just isn't right."

"Don't leave me," she said. "Please don't leave me alone."

In truth, the housekeeper's departure was inevitable. Funds were running desperately low, and Nancy had spent the last few weeks working up the courage to tell the only woman she still considered a friend. It was something of a relief, she thought, Inez deciding to part ways on her own terms. But as she watched the woman who had been their housekeeper turn the handle of the front door for the last time, she was overcome with the feeling of sadness and the loss of something she knew would never return.

"Wait," she said, ducking into Byron's study and returning a moment later. "I have something for you."

It was the last of the cash she'd had stashed away in a safety deposit box. It was for a rainy day, she'd told her husband when they rented the box.

"I can't, Nancy." Inez's face betrayed her secret pity for the sad woman who, in the last few months, had aged more than in the previous decade.

"Please," she said. "Take it home for your grandkids. Buy them something nice."

"Oh, those kids don't need anything. I spoil them with love."

Nancy was sure she did. "If you need anything, a job reference maybe, don't hesitate to ask."

"Same to you, dear."

And just like that she was gone.

Nancy fought back the urge to run to the window and watch her climb into the cab. It would only hurt more, she thought, as she slumped to the floor, back against the heavy door, and cried.

Her quiet sobs were interrupted moments later by a loud knock. Maybe it was Inez, returning to say she'd had second thoughts about leaving.

She jumped to her feet and swung the door open without pausing to peek through the peephole. Inez had only just left. Who else could it be?

Whatever fleeting hope she'd felt disappeared when she saw the camera and a young woman in a trim suit holding out a microphone.

"Nancy Hardaway," said the woman, "is it true a young boy died in your house? What can you tell us about the circumstances of his death?"

"I'm sorry," she said. "I've been advised by my attorney not to make any comments to the media."

She was about to swing the door closed when the young reporter put one foot across the threshold. "Does this have anything to do with your husband's recent conviction?"

Nancy wondered if there was anything these people wouldn't do to fill a time slot.

"What about the dead nanny?" The reporter took another step forward, the camera operator sliding up beside her to fill the open doorframe. "Is it true this is the second suspicious death under your roof?"

Mr. Bennett had told her not to respond. It'll only encourage them, he'd said. But as the woman in the suit edged closer and closer, Nancy felt the sum of her frustrations, forced down into some dark place deep inside her, come bubbling to the surface.

"Fuck you," she said, the words rising up and spilling from her throat before she could do anything to stop them. "Fuck you people with your cameras and your ridiculous questions! Why can't you just leave me alone?"

The reporter looked genuinely shocked, struggling for a moment to compose herself before pressing on with another question.

Nancy never gave her the opportunity.

She dug her heels in and shoved hard, forcing the reporter back over the threshold and into the crouching camera operator. They went down together in a tangled mess of flailing arms and expensive equipment, the camera breaking into several pieces on impact.

"That's assault!" said the reporter, before turning to the camera operator. "Did you get that on film? Please tell me you got it."

He was too busy fumbling with pieces of the broken camera to respond. "Shit! This better not come out of my paycheck."

With the door clear, Nancy slammed it shut and turned the deadbolt. It serves them right, she thought, harassing people in their own homes. Besides, they were clearly trespassing. Let them show the footage. What did she care?

Her sudden act of defiance had lifted her spirits, and she was feeling rather good about herself as she poured a drink and took a seat, not on the sofa, but behind the desk in her husband's study. The cellphone in her pocket rang before she could raise the glass to her lips. Mr. Bennett's face, framed by one of his expensive suits, lit up the screen.

"Ugh," she said to the empty room. "What now?"

She took a sip before answering. Lord only knows, she thought, how much money her husband had paid that snake of a man. He could wait a few more seconds.

"What is it, Anthony? I'm in the middle of something important."

The lawyer sounded surprised, as if he couldn't imagine she had anything important to do. "I've got good news. The judge granted our petition for Byron's release. I'm on my way to the jail as we speak."

"He's coming home?"

"For now," said the lawyer. "If all goes well I'll have him back to you in time for dinner."

It had been a long time since she'd last cooked, but with Inez gone she'd have to figure out something to prepare on her own. It didn't matter. She'd missed her husband more than she would have imagined, even the stupid way he snored and tossed around in bed, and she would be happy to have him back in the house. "Thank you, Anthony."

"Don't thank me too much. It's only temporary, just until he goes back to court for sentencing."

The last part didn't matter. At least for now she wouldn't be sleeping alone.

"Nancy—" He was still in the same suit he was wearing when they'd taken him off to jail, and had only to say her name to send her bursting into tears.

She threw herself at him and wrapped her arms around his shoulders. "Oh Byron, it's been just awful without you here."

"I'm home now," he said. "I'm home."

When the tears had dried, he excused himself and went upstairs to kiss Nora. Nancy finished up dinner—a simple penne pasta with canned tomato sauce—and lit a single white candle at the center of the kitchen table.

It was almost romantic, the two of them eating together as the candle flame bounced and flickered. If he was disappointed by the simple meal, the way he devoured his plate didn't show it.

"I hope it's okay," she said. "I never was much use in the kitchen."

"It's no secret—you were always too busy entertaining guests to bother with cooking." He reached across the table and took her hands. "It's the best meal I've had since they took me away in handcuffs. Never go to jail, Nancy. The food is awful."

She wanted to laugh at his stupid joke, but instead the tears returned to her tired eyes. "What are we going to do, Byron? This house—where are we going to go?"

"Do you remember Stephanie?"

She nodded as she wiped away the tears. Stephanie was his sister. Nancy had met her only once, at their wedding. The only thing she remembered about Stephanie was that she lived in California with her husband, a little-known music producer, whose only real credit was a Christmas album for a popular teenage pop star. Nonetheless, it was a major hit, played on radio stations coast to coast during the holiday season.

"I talked to her while I was in jail. She and her husband bought a lake house up in Oregon a few years back. Haven't used it once, and the place is just sitting empty. She said you could stay there with Nora. They'd actually be glad to have someone looking after things."

"Oregon? Who do I know in Oregon?"

"It's only temporary, at least until I get released from prison. Think of it like a fresh start—a new life away from Boston."

More like a banishment, she thought. But maybe a fresh start was exactly what they needed, far away from the things that reminded her of the glamorous life she'd once lived. And there was something else—an image she couldn't erase from her mind. It came to her each night as she drifted off to sleep—the dead boy in the bodybag and those red eyes, glowing in the dark.

He squeezed her hands. "Are you okay?"

"Yes," she said. "I'm fine."

"It's the boy, isn't it? I wish I could have been here to help you through that."

But you weren't, she thought. You were in jail, and I went to bed alone at night with the screams of the caretaker playing over and over in my head. "Can we talk about something else." She was tired of thinking about it—so dreadfully tired.

"Sure," he said. "But Nancy—"

"Yes?"

"I'm sorry."

"Do you remember the Driscolls?" She laughed as she poured herself another glass of scotch. Was it her second— or maybe it was her third? No matter. She was happy for the distraction.

Byron smiled. "How could I forget Bob and Diane?"

"Denise," she said.

"Are you sure? I could have sworn it was Diane."

"No, I'm quite sure it was Denise. We had tennis lessons together every Thursday while you and Bob were busy at the office. She had a thing for the tennis pro. He was Czech, or was it Polish? Either way, Denise couldn't get enough of him in those little white shorts."

It was Byron's turn to refill his glass. They'd drifted into the study after dinner, swapping old stories over drinks as if the events of the last year had never happened. "Oh right, Denise. We shared a suite with them on that company trip to Mexico."

Nancy remembered it well. She and Byron had been married only the year before. He was a much younger man then, so eager to climb the corporate ladder. The trip to Mexico had been some kind of half-disguised business re- treat, but on the last day they took a pleasure cruise from Puerto Vallarta. "Bob got so drunk on piña coladas he fell off the boat."

Byron laughed. "Poor bastard was bobbing around in the Pacific for a good ten minutes while they brought the boat around. I thought he was going to drown."

"Yes," she said, "but the best part was Denise shouting 'shark!' over the railing as the crew threw him a life preserver. I'll never forget the look on his face."

"She was brutal, that Denise."

They laughed so hard Nancy thought she might pee her pants. "You know, Denise wasn't the only one with a thing for the tennis pro."

"Oh, really?"

"It was only natural." Nancy giggled. "He had a lot of balls."

Byron sipped his scotch, eyeing her over the edge of the glass. "I could be your tennis pro."

"Why Byron Hardaway, is that some kind of proposal?"

She could remember Bob and Denise Driscoll and the trip to Mexico. She could remember the long hours in the courthouse, and the innocent face of the caretaker's son as he played with his toy cars on the verandah, but she couldn't remember the last time Byron had made love to her with so much passion. Surely, she thought, it was some time before Nora had been born, before they'd started trying for a baby and sex had become just another routine.

He'd taken his time, starting with gentle kisses on her neck and then working his way down to the warm place between her thighs. More than once she thought she might climax, but he pulled back, delivering more tender kisses that sent chills running over her skin.

Finally, when she could wait no longer, he entered her. They moved in rhythmic motion, up and down like the cascading waves of an ocean, until they collapsed together on the mattress, two bodies breathing heavily in the dark.

"I love you," he said, as he placed one last kiss upon her forehead.

She feel asleep with his arm around her, the final thought passing through her mind as she drifted off was that she believed him—he loved her and somehow everything would be okay.

His arm was still around her when she woke up in the morning. But something was different. His warm embrace had been replaced by cold and clammy skin.

"Byron?" She gave him a nudge and he slid over onto his back, limp arms flopping down at his sides. "Wake up, Byron."

She knew he wasn't going to wake up. The look in his eyes, the blank stare on his face, was the same as that of the nanny when she'd found her sprawled on the floor of the nursery.

Her husband was dead.

TWENTY-FOUR

They met Vladislav at the tavern and fled the city with no time for an explanation. It had been self-defense, the killing of Ion and the man with the axe, but they were in a foreign land, surrounded by foreign people, who were unlikely to tolerate the slaying of two of their own by strangers from the north.

They moved quickly, stopping only to rest for a few hours at a time. Ten days had passed, maybe more, when they came upon the empty village where they'd been captured by Yegor and his band of wild men.

Bogdan had expected they might see them there, lurking in the forest with their peculiar masks, intent on some kind of retribution for their fallen leader. But if they were near, they remained out of sight. He wondered if they had made good on their promise to become farmers.

It's the long journey back, Svyatoslav had told to him one night as they set out again into the dark, when the heart aches most for home. Perhaps he was right, but as the days passed Bogdan couldn't help feeling a mounting sense of dread. He imagined them returning to an empty village, not unlike the one they had passed on the trail, dead bodies and barren cupboards the only things left behind by those who had given up hope.

And so he was relieved, as they approached the outskirts of their village on a late summer day, to find folks working in the fields.

"It's Bogdan!" A sturdy woman wielding a hoe stood and peered out over tall crops, one hand shielding her eyes from the sun. "Fetch the priest! Bogdan the Great has returned!"

They had been gone two months, and were greeted with smiles and cheers by the men and women of the village. The old priest, who was looking better than he had when they'd left, took Bogdan in his arms.

"I never doubted," said the old man. "I was certain God would return you safe. But what of the evil spirit? We've suffered not a single death since you left."

Bogdan was happy to see the innocent faces of the village children, running in circles around their parent's legs, but he was exhausted from the journey, more exhausted than he imagined any one person could ever be. "We shall talk, but first I must rest."

"Yes," said the priest. "Go and rest easy, my son."

He slept for two days, waking only to relieve himself and eat the hearty soup that Svyatoslav's wife carried to his house in the evenings.

On the second night, the priest came to join him at his table. "Tell me, my dearest friend, tell me of your journey and what you have seen."

Bogdan raised an eyebrow as he broke off a piece of bread and dipped it in the soup. "Have you not already spoken to Svyatoslav?"

The priest smiled. "I tried. He says I must speak only to Bogdan the Great."

"Very well," he said. "What do you want to know?"

"Everything. Tell me everything."

They ate their soup and he spoke of cannibals, of the city that was both the filthiest and most beautiful thing he'd ever seen. He told the story of Vlad Ţepeş the Impaler, and the treachery of Ion. When he'd almost reached the end, he crossed the room and returned with the silver stake they'd found in the Impaler's grave.

The priest turned it over in his hands, the shiny metal reflecting the flames in the hearth. "What is it?"

"They drove it through his heart, some two centuries before our time. When we found him there was nothing but a box of dust."

"I don't understand," said the priest. "If he was sent to Hell by a stake in the heart, how is it that he's continued to ravage us for hundreds of years?"

It was a question Bogdan had considered for much of the long road home—one for which he was only able to reach a single conclusion. "Because they were not successful in sending him to Hell, only in driving him away from the city."

"But his body—you said it had turned to dust."

"Yes." Bogdan scraped soup from the bottom of the bowl with his spoon. "He must have found a new one."

The old man sighed. In a single moment, the weariness of the past returned to his eyes. "There's another matter," he said. "I'm afraid it can't wait."

"What is it, priest?"

"It's your son, Bogdan. He needs a name for the baptism, something made all the more pressing if what you've said is true. I've been patient, but now, as the spiritual leader of our community, I must insist."

"Kyrill," he said. "I'll call him Kyrill."

A tiny spark returned to the priest's eyes. "Bless you, Bogdan. You've given a sad old man some small measure of happiness."

It was a humble ceremony. Bogdan carried his son, who had been well-kept and grown larger in his absence, to the sanctuary of the wooden church.

The priest lit a candle and read aloud from the Book of Matthew. "Let the little children come to me, and do not hinder them, for the Kingdom of Heaven belongs to such as these."

Svyatoslav and his wife were presented as godparents, each promising to love and cherish the child as their own. Bogdan was sure he saw Svyatoslav cry.

Then it was his turn.

"What name have you chosen for this child?"

"Kyrill," he said. "Son of Bogdan."

The priest made the sign of the cross on the boy's forehead and repeated the name. "I baptize you, Kyrill, son of Bogdan, in the name of the Father, the Son, and the Holy Spirit. May you know God's love forever."

The whole of the village, at least those who had survived, turned out to celebrate the baptism. The harvest would be upon them soon, and there would be enough food to last another winter. Though it had only been two months since seven of their own had perished in a single night, all were convinced the evil spirit had been dispelled, and that the many tragedies which had befallen their village would trouble them no longer.

All except for Bogdan.

Svyatoslav sat beside him, struggling to balance a beer in his hand as he swung his heavy legs over the bench. "Come now, my friend. Surely you can be happy for one night."

"It won't last," he said.

The big man put his beer on the table and got to work loading his pipe. "Nothing ever does."

The cool morning air chilled his skin—the first sign of fall. He'd woken up early, and was alone as he strolled past quiet little homes. Only a rooster was crowing. They were sleeping it off, he thought. Most of the village had stayed up well into the night. Even Svyatoslav, widely known for his ability to out-drink almost anyone, had to be carried off to his bed.

He reached the edge of the village and found the tree where he'd been tied and left to die. His sacrifice had never truly ended. It continued one day after the next, and as he stood staring up at the branches, he wondered if it might continue this way forever.

The answer came in the form of a woman's cries, rising up and spilling out of a nearby house.

By the time the village came to life, three more were dead. Vladislav was among them.

TWENTY-FIVE

"Nancy Hardaway, my name is Detective Jim Davies of the Boston Police Department." He wore a trim mustache and drank coffee from a styrofoam cup. "I'm very sorry for your loss."

"Why am I here?" She'd been taken down to the police station in the back of a squad car, not long after the ambulance left with her husband's body.

"I can assure you it's all standard procedure."

She'd seen enough television dramas to know it's rarely a good sign whenever a cop says something is standard procedure. "Detective, my husband has just passed away. I should be at home with my daughter."

"This won't take long."

She crossed her arms and stared around the room. It was one of those small rooms with a low ceiling and a glass mirror on the wall. She imagined this was the same type of room where they'd taken Byron after his arrest, and she wondered who might be watching from the other side of the one-way mirror. "Do I need a lawyer?"

The detective took another sip of his coffee. "You're welcome to call your lawyer, Nancy. But then we have to wait for them to come, and everything gets much more complicated. I just want to ask some simple questions. Is that okay?"

She thought she was stupid for asking. Anyone who had ever been brought to one of these rooms needed a lawyer. But she was tired, and her head spun from the shock of waking up to find her husband dead. And so it was easy to make the same careless mistake so many others before her had made. "Okay," she said, "as long as it doesn't take too long."

Detective Davies smiled. "That's better. Could you please state your name for the record?"

"Nancy—Nancy Hardaway."

"See, that wasn't so hard. Would you like some coffee, Nancy? Maybe some tea?"

"No, thank you." She wasn't planning to stay long enough for coffee.

"Smart choice. The coffee around here is terrible."

"Detective, I really must insist we move this along."

Another sip of coffee. "Right, of course. Where were you last night?"

"I was at home with my husband. As I'm sure you're well aware, he'd just been released from jail. The trial was all over the news."

"Yes," he said. "I'm aware. And were you with him the whole night?"

She nodded. "I made dinner, penne pasta, and we went to bed together sometime around midnight."

The detective was taking notes on a yellow pad of paper. "Was that the last time you saw him? What I mean to ask is, did either of you wake up at any point in the night? Maybe you went to the bathroom, or down to the kitchen for a snack?"

"I fell asleep in his arms, and that's exactly how I woke up in the morning." It had been the first time she'd felt truly loved by him in a long time, and the memory of it nearly sent her into tears. But she stiffened up in her seat. She wouldn't give this stupid detective, whoever he was, the satisfaction of seeing her cry.

"I see. Thank you, Nancy. That's very good. Who else was in the house last night?"

"My daughter Nora, and the nanny."

"Right. What can you tell me about the nanny? Let's start with her name."

"Iryna," she said.

He wrote it down on his yellow pad. "And her last name?"

She was embarrassed to admit she couldn't remember Iryna's last name. It was one of those difficult Slavic words she'd always had trouble pronouncing. Was it Petrovich? No, that wasn't right. "I'm sorry," she said. "I can't remember."

The detective raised an eyebrow. "It's rather strange, don't you think? This woman cares for your child and you can't remember her last name? You must have conducted a thorough background check before bringing her into your home."

In fact, she had done no such thing, and as she considered his question she realized just how little she really knew about the woman who spent so much time with her daughter. There was only one thing she knew for certain. Iryna, for whatever reason, had lied about her professional references on her résumé—and in all of the confusion surrounding Byron's arrest she'd chosen to overlook it.

"We'll need to speak with her," said the detective.

"Yes, of course." She wondered if they might find something awful hidden in Iryna's past.

"Are you sure you don't want something to drink, Mrs. Hardaway? You look a bit flushed."

"I'm upset," she said. "My husband is dead. How much longer is this going to take?"

"I know this must be difficult and I appreciate your co-operation. Just a few more questions." He pulled a large photo from a manila folder and slid it across the table. "Who is this woman?"

It was a photo of their first nanny, smiling and full of life. Nancy guessed the photo was taken some time before the woman had come to work for them. "She was our first nanny."

"She died in your home, did she not?"

"Yes."

"How?"

"I'm sorry?"

"How did she die?"

She didn't like the way he asked the question, the forceful tone of his voice. Something about it made her feel defensive, as if she had suddenly found herself on trial. "I'm not sure. As far as I know, the medical examiner was unable to determine a specific cause of death."

"Hmm." He scratched more notes in his yellow pad and then produced another photo. "What about this one? How did he die?"

It was the caretaker's son, cold and stiff on a stainless steel autopsy table.

"I don't understand," she said. "Why are you doing this?"

Still another photo. This time it was her husband, just as she'd found him in bed. "And this one?" said the detective. "What about this one?"

She wanted to run. She wanted to scream. She wanted to punch him in the face. But she did none of those things. Instead, she took a deep breath and looked him straight in the eyes. "I want my lawyer."

"Are you insane?" Mr. Bennett had come straight from the squash courts. It was the first time Nancy had ever seen him in anything other than a suit. He was quick to give his condolences before unleashing his anger on the detective. "In all my years as an attorney, I've never seen such malicious harassment. This poor woman just lost her husband, and you want to throw about baseless accusations?"

The detective appeared unfazed. "I've got three mysterious deaths, all under the same roof. And the only person who was present for all three is your client."

"It's a stretch," said the attorney. "I can't believe you're even entertaining this—never mind the ill-timed and hugely insensitive manner of your interrogation. What could Mrs. Hardaway possibly have to gain from her husband's death?"

"How about one million dollars?"

"You're joking."

"On the contrary," he said. "Were you aware of Mr. Hardaway's life insurance policy?"

"Of course. I'm his lawyer—was his lawyer. But what does that have to do with the nanny or the boy?"

"See, that's where things get fuzzy. Look, I'll cut to the chase. We opened an investigation into Mrs. Hardaway after the boy died. It never went anywhere, at least not until to-day. Two deaths is suspicious. Three deaths is a pattern." He let the last part hang in the air for a moment before continu-ing. "The way I see it, we have two choices. Your client can go ahead and confess, in which case I'd be happy to clear up those fuzzy details, or we can all hunker down and see how this plays out."

Nancy thought maybe it was all just a dream, a night-mare from which she would wake to find Byron still sleeping peacefully beside her. All she wanted was to go home and kiss her baby. Nora had already been left without a father. Would she also have to grow up without a mother? "Why would I confess? I haven't—"

Mr. Bennett interrupted. "Detective, is my client under arrest?"

"Well, no. Not yet."

"Great. Which way to the nearest exit?"

The lawyer drove her home in his BMW. "They don't have anything," he said, as he left her at the front door. "Don't worry about it. You've been through so much already. I'll handle everything."

She muttered something like 'thank you' and dragged herself across the threshold. The police were the last of her worries. The night before, she'd believed her husband when he said everything would be okay. Prison would only be temporary, nothing more than a very long business trip. But now he was gone—gone and never coming back.

Iryna was loading Nora into a pram at the bottom of the stairs. "Nancy, I'm so sorry. I'm afraid I've never been good at these things, but if you need anything, please don't hesitate to ask."

"Can I hold her?"

"Of course, dear."

She couldn't remember the last time she had held her baby. It felt good cradling Nora's warm little body in her arms. She kissed the top of her head and Nora giggled. She has Byron's eyes, she thought, as she lowered her back into the pram.

"We were just going out for some fresh air," said the nanny. "Why don't you rest for a while? I'll make you some tea when we come back."

"Sure. Yes." Everything since the police station had been a blur. Though she'd slept well the night before, her body felt heavy. She was exhausted, and after the nanny left with Nora, she fell to the floor and sobbed—big, wet tears rolling down her face and pooling on the black and white tiles of the hallway floor.

How long she remained on the floor she couldn't say, but after some time she gathered her strength and climbed the stairs. She'd intended on going straight to bed, perhaps with one of the little blue pills she'd been prescribed for such moments, but as she passed the nanny's door she paused.

Her mind raced back to the police station and the detective's questions. It was true, she had been present for all three deaths under her roof. But the nanny, who she knew so little about, had also been present for the deaths of both the caretaker's son and her husband.

An image flashed through her mind—the memory of Iryna knocking on their door at the stroke of midnight.

"I hear you're in need of a nanny," the old woman had said in her unplaceable accent.

Nancy had always believed in respecting privacy, but Byron was dead and everything had changed. She pushed the door open and peered into the woman's room. "Who are you?"

The nightstand was empty save for a pair of reading glasses and a small copy of the Bible.

She opened the wardrobe and found the woman's frumpy, gray clothes hanging in a tidy row. She'd almost closed the doors when she noticed the old leather bag Iryna had arrived with, flattened and placed inconspicuously on the top shelf.

It too was empty, but as Nancy ran her fingers over the smooth leather she felt a long, hard shape hidden in the bottom beneath the lining.

It's wouldn't be right, she thought, to damage the woman's bag. But this was still her house, at least for a while longer, and the time for common courtesy had long since passed.

She went to the bathroom and returned with a pair of delicate scissors, her curiosity overwhelming any last doubts she had about invading the old nanny's privacy.

The scissors made quick work of the lining, and in less than a minute she'd slid the object from its hiding place.

She held it up for closer inspection. It was metal, and shiny, and sharpened to a point at one end.

She was so absorbed in her work she didn't hear the front door open and close, didn't hear the footsteps on the stairs, didn't notice the figure standing in the open doorway behind her.

"Nancy?"

She was startled by the sound of her own name, and when she spun around Iryna was there, arms folded over her chest. "I'm sorry," she said, holding up the metal object in her hand. "But I had to know. Who are you?"

If the old woman was upset, she didn't show it. She only sighed and took a seat on the edge of the bed. "It's time," she said. "We need to talk."

TWENTY-SIX

Hunger gnawed at his stomach. His vision blurred and dimmed from lack of sleep. He'd been wandering alone through the woods for two days.

"What will you do?" Svyatoslav had said to him as he set off from the village. The big man was desperate for vengeance. He'd loved Vladislav like a son.

"I don't know, but I'm not coming back until that vile monster is finally dead."

"Then I'll go with you."

"No," he'd said. "I must do it alone."

Despite the protests of his oldest friend, he'd stormed off without bothering to pack any food. He carried only the clothes on his back, the knife he wore at his side, and the silver stake he'd recovered from the grave of the one they called Vlad the Impaler.

For two full days and nights, he walked without stopping to rest. On the second night, he tripped over a snarled branch and twisted his ankle—but he climbed to his feet and continued, limping along as he went.

He drank from small streams, and when there were no streams he drank from puddles. The muddy water made him sick, but still he didn't rest.

On more than one occasion, he was sure the evil spirit watched him—taunted him. Ever since the night of his ceremonial sacrifice, their fates had been forever twisted together, as inseparable as the seasons which ebbed and flowed and ran into one another. Bogdan didn't have to see him. He could feel him. Now he was very close.

As dusk fell on his third night of wandering the forest, he was overtaken by a ravenous hunger. If only he could catch a rabbit, he thought, or some other creature, he might fill his belly. Finally, when he thought he could stand it no longer, he found a patch of mushrooms at the base of a mighty oak and ate.

They were bitter, but he was happy to have something in his stomach. He settled against the tree and closed his eyes. Just a minute, he thought. I'll only rest for a few minutes.

When he opened his eyes again the forest had changed. Trees swirled and pulsed. Snarled branches, their silhouettes dark against the night sky, reached down as if to grab him. He wondered if it was only a dream—perhaps he was still asleep, the evil spirit hovering over his body.

He tried to stand and got sick. He wasn't dreaming. It was the mushrooms, which had transformed the forest into something much darker—sinister.

A voice called to him from behind the trees. It was the voice of an angel. It was the voice of his beloved Yekaterina. "Bogdan? Where are you, Bogdan?"

"I'm here," he said, steadying himself and pushing deeper into the forest. She was out there, somewhere in the black night, and he would find her.

But no matter how far he followed, the voice moved farther away.

"Please," he said. "Don't go."

"I'm here," she cried. "I'm here, Bogdan. Where are you, my love?"

It continued this way throughout the night. Tears rolled down his face and a great thirst clawed at his throat. Branches scratched and bloodied his skin, but he gave them no mind. He had to find her, even if it cost him his life.

He couldn't be sure how long he had followed her voice, only that he was tired, so very tired, and afraid he wouldn't be able to continue much longer.

Then he did something he had never done before.

He collapsed to his knees, closed his eyes, and prayed aloud. "God, please help me."

Perhaps it was God, or the mushrooms, or nothing more than the approaching dawn, but as he teetered on the precipice of losing hope, a single ray of sunlight filtered through the twisted branches of the trees and lit his face.

That's when he saw it—a tiny stone hut, not much more than a pile of loose rocks, only a short distance from where he'd dropped to his knees. And he knew, beyond any doubt, that whatever fate God might have ordained for him waited inside.

The wooden door had long since rotted away. The space inside was dark, not yet illuminated by the first rays of the early morning sun. He stood in the open doorway for what might have been several minutes, until at last he found the courage to cross the threshold.

His eyes struggled to readjust to the enveloping darkness, but even then he could see the human figure slumped over in the corner.

"Hello?" He moved closer, unsure if they were dead or only sleeping.

He remembered the others, the people of his village who he'd buried in the expanding cemetery at the edge of the forest. Even in winter, with its cold and dry air, there had been the familiar smell—the smell of death. If the person slumped in the corner was dead, there was no foul smell to give it away.

He was close enough now to make out the face of a young man, untarnished and fresh, without a single wrinkle or blemish. But though the face was fresh, the clothes he wore were old, like something Bogdan's great-grandfather might have worn, and covered in a thick layer of dust.

He reminded himself to breathe. His heart pounded furiously against his ribs. Blood pulsed up and beat in his ears. And there was something else, a tingling in the air and on his skin, like the tingling sensation of a nearby storm.

With great care and concentration, steadying his hand and breath so as not to make a sound, he slid the silver stake from its hiding place in the pocket of his trousers—wrapped his fingers tightly around the shaft and raised it above his head.

There was only one last thing to do. His free hand reached out into the darkness and tapped the slumped figure on the shoulder.

Breathe, he told himself. Breathe.

For a moment, he was sure the mouth moved. It was only one corner, raising ever so slightly before returning to its original position—or was it a trick of the light?

I've gone mad, he thought.

But he wasn't mad. He wasn't crazy.

The eyes flicked open—two red eyes burning like hot coals in a fire.

This time there was no doubt. He lifted the stake higher, and then, in a single violent motion, plunged it deep into the young man's chest.

Now it was the mouth that opened—a primal scream erupting from stretched lips.

Bogdan stumbled backward and fell to his knees. The noise was deafening, like the sound of a hundred pigs being slaughtered. He raised both hands to shield his ears and felt thin trickles of warm blood ooze gently down his cheeks.

And then it was over.

The young man's body, long dead but preserved in a state of near perfection by the presence of the evil spirit, crumbled to the floor of the hut in a pile of dust.

TWENTY-SEVEN

Iryna paused to sip her tea, the third cup she'd poured since beginning the story. When she'd returned the cup to its little dish, she continued. "And so the evil spirit of Vlad the Impaler was banished forever from their lands. There were those who still doubted, as was only natural, but when the eve of the annual sacrifice passed without a single death, they knew they'd finally been saved.

"Yet Bogdan grew ever more restless. He'd spent his whole life preparing to die, and had found in his battle against the evil spirit a reason to live. With his enemy defeated, there was nothing left to do but sow the fields and father his motherless son."

Nancy shifted her weight on the leather sofa. They'd been in the study for two hours, Iryna telling her what she could only assume was some kind of Eastern European folk legend—tales of vampires and a reluctant hero, Bogdan the Great. It had been wildly entertaining, a welcome distraction from her husband's death, but she wondered if there was some deeper intention behind the telling of the story. The old woman didn't really expect her to believe the silver stake —the very same one she still clutched in her left hand—had been used to slay a vampire some three hundred years before. Or did she?

"Oh, I know it's all very hard to believe," Iryna said, as if somehow reading her mind. "Would you like to hear how it ends?"

She sipped from her own cup of tea and nodded.

"Where was I?" The old woman stared up at the ceiling for a moment, as though recalling a distant memory. "Oh, right. Bogdan had grown terribly restless, so when word reached the village of a ship departing the Black Sea coast for the New World, he took his son and left.

"It was a dangerous journey, but each day was filled with new discoveries—a world which he'd only ever imagined. He marveled in wonder at the majestic domes of Istanbul as they sailed the shallow waters of the Bosphorus. He fought bravely to repel an attack by pirates off the Barbary Coast of Africa. And in the long, idle months spent crossing the Atlantic, he thought of her—the woman he'd left behind in the old country. He knew she was with him in spirit. But unbeknownst to poor Bogdan, she wasn't the only one."

Iryna took another sip of tea. "After half a year at sea, they came to shore in Newfoundland, where Bogdan found work as a fisherman in a small settlement populated by those who spoke his language. It was hard work, but his journey had instilled within him a deep love for the sea. His son, the one they called Kyrill, grew strong and healthy. And so for a time he was happy.

"But happiness, as you well know, Mrs. Hardaway, is a fragile thing. Sometime during the first winter, a series of mysterious deaths struck the settlement. Several fishermen, robust and hardy men not easily prone to illness, were found dead in their beds. Bogdan knew it could only mean one thing. The evil spirit of Vlad the Impaler, full of energy from the souls he'd gorged upon in the old country, had somehow come to follow him to the New World."

Nancy thought she was beginning to understand. At first it had only been an inkling, a peculiar idea floating around in the back of her mind. "Iryna, are you saying my husband was killed by a vampire?"

"Yes." The old woman looked her squarely in the eyes and let the word hang for a moment. "But not just any vampire. Your husband was killed by the evil spirit of Vlad Țepeș, the Impaler."

"And the nanny? The caretaker's son?"

Iryna nodded.

Nancy wondered if the woman's elaborate story was some kind of cruel joke meant to torment her. She considered tossing her out on the curb, or even calling that police detective—what was his name?

"You've seen him," said the nanny. "Haven't you?"

She didn't want it to be true. If it was true, it would mean she was just as insane as the nanny. She had certainly seen something—a pair of red eyes staring back at her on the night the caretaker's son had died. And then there was the visitor, the one who came at night in her dreams. "But how did you know?"

The old woman smiled. A gentle warmth radiated from behind her blue eyes. "If it's not too much, dear, I'd like to finish the story. Perhaps it will make everything clear."

Clear. It was the last word Iryna said that Nancy clung to desperately. She had come this far. It was too late to turn back. Whatever Iryna had to say, she wanted to hear it.

The old woman took Nancy's silence as permission to resume. "Our poor Bogdan, dear sweet Bogdan, was locked in battle yet again with the evil spirit. And once again, he emerged victorious. But no matter how many times Bogdan killed his mortal host, the evil spirit found a new body in which to rest. On and on it went, until Bogdan was too old and tired to fight. And so it was Kyrill who took up the silver stake, and picked up where his father left off.

"It has continued this way in my family for nearly three-hundred years—the silver stake passing from one generation to the next—until finally it arrived in my possession." Iryna sighed, a long, slow exhale that made her old face look even more weary. "I'm afraid I'm the last of us."

The story had come full circle. If Nancy was to believe the old woman, she was the last in a long line of vampire hunters, whose story had brought her knocking on the Hardaway's door in the middle of the night. "You're not really a nanny, are you?"

"I'm afraid not, my dear. I regret concealing my true identity. It was necessary, so as not to arouse suspicion. The evil spirit is very near."

A year earlier, Nancy's only concern was what to wear to the latest charity fundraiser. Now Byron was dead, along with the first nanny and the caretaker's son. Her world had flipped upside down, and if helping Iryna was the only way to set it right, so be it.

A single question remained—the same question asked time and time again by those people who find themselves in impossible situations. "Why us? Why would the evil spirit come here?"

"He chose you."

"But why?"

"Please forgive me, Nancy. What I'm about to say will sting. You see, the evil spirit was drawn to your household. You share a similar energy."

She wondered what the old woman meant. "Similar energy? In what way?"

"You're vampires, Nancy—you and Byron."

"Have you totally lost your mind?" If she was indeed a vampire, nobody had ever bothered telling her. And Byron was dead. Weren't vampires supposed to live forever? Perhaps Iryna really had gone mad, and it was all just the ranting of a crazy old woman.

"Not literal vampires, of course. But you are vampires nonetheless—parasites sucking the life from those around you. How many millions did Byron steal? How many families were sent to ruin? And for what? Another fur coat or diamond necklace?"

Nancy wanted to be angry, but she knew the old woman was right. They were vampires—they had bled people dry and provided nothing of value in return. Now it was her turn to suffer. Her eyes became wet and she thought she might cry.

Iryna smiled again. "Take heart, my dear. It's never too late to do the right thing."

Something about the woman's smile comforted her, and this time she knew exactly what Iryna meant. Although she didn't yet understand what it might be, she had a role to play. She was a part of the story, and together they would write the last chapter. "Okay, how do we kill him?"

"You mean her."

"What?"

Iryna sighed, the same heavy sigh as before. "The sweet child who sleeps in your nursery is not your daughter, but rather the evil spirit of Vlad Țepeș—the terrible monster of so many legends."

Nancy gasped for air. Her vision blurred and the room spun and twisted in all directions. It was the same familiar feeling she'd had at the courthouse when Byron was found guilty, and for a moment she thought she might black out.

"Easy, dear." Iryna leaned forward and placed a steadying hand on her knee. "Breathe."

She did as the old woman told her, and in another minute the room stopped spinning. "Are you saying you want to kill Nora?"

"No," said Iryna. "Not me. It must be you—the one who carried Vlad's spirit in your womb."

This has all gone too far, she thought. Stories and legends were one thing, but now the old woman was suggesting the murder of an innocent child. She dropped the silver stake and watched it roll toward Iryna's feet. "It's time for you to leave."

Iryna was undeterred. "Think, Nancy. Did something happen not long before Nora was born? Something strange or unusual?"

A deep chill ran down her spine and settled in her hands and feet. She remembered the nightmare she'd had a month before the doctors confirmed her pregnancy—the same dark figure who'd revealed himself the night the caretaker's poor son died, and who she'd welcomed as a lover in her dreams.

They'd called her pregnancy a miracle.

A miracle.

They were wrong. It was a curse.

"We can end this, Nancy." There was something rushed and nervous about the way the old woman spoke. "For three centuries we've pursued him, the descendants of Bogdan the

Great. And for three centuries he's slipped away, jumping from one dead corpse to another, always one step ahead. But never before has he joined his spirit with a living, breathing human. It was a risk, a gamble, the reckless pursuit of a form in which he might the walk the earth again. He's made himself weak—vulnerable."

"Will it work?"

"It has to work. I'm the last one left. Bogdan's line dies with me."

Iryna was right about the Hardaways. Nancy wasn't a good person. But she'd never murdered anyone, not least of all her own flesh and blood. "She's my daughter."

"She killed your husband. She killed that boy. And she'll kill again and again unless you, Nancy Hardaway, do something to stop her. This is your chance to do something good, something right. Send Vlad Țepeș to Hell."

Iryna nudged the stake with her shoe. It rolled back to Nancy's feet and she bent down, picked it up.

She was outside of her body now, watching herself tighten her grip around the cold metal, watching herself follow the old woman up the stairs to the nursery. Was it real? Yes, it was real. She was going to kill a baby.

"I've drugged her," said the woman who had once been nothing more than an eccentric old nanny.

The room was dark, lit only by the light of a streetlamp filtering in through the window. Nancy crept slowly toward the crib, convinced she would see a monster. But there was only a baby—the same baby for whom she'd endured seventeen hours of labor and a caesarean section—the same little girl who'd giggled when she kissed her on the forehead, a dollop of whip cream hanging from her tiny chin.

"Do it, Nancy. Do it and save us all."

She had always been a terrible mother, more concerned with herself, or what other people might think, than Nora's well-being. One quick thrust of the stake and it would all be over. The police would come for her, of that she had no doubt. But did it matter? She had no husband, no home, and soon enough, no daughter.

Iryna hovered over her shoulder. "Think of the lives you'll save. You'll be a hero—if not in the eyes of men, then most certainly in the eyes of the Lord. As Bogdan sacrificed himself to save the village, so too must you sacrifice your only child so that others might live."

She raised the stake above her head.

"Quickly, my dear! If she wakes it's all over."

Too late.

Nora opened her eyes.

"Do it," said the old woman. "Do it now!"

Nancy remembered the time she told her husband she wished their daughter had never been born. The moment had finally come. She would be a mother no longer. Her hand trembled as she raised the stake higher still.

But before she could strike, a single word passed between Baby Nora's tiny lips. "Mommy."

Mommy.

Nobody had ever called her mommy.

Iryna gripped her arm from behind. Nancy was surprised by the old woman's strength.

"We'll do it together."

There was no more time for hesitation. No more time for doubt. For the first time in Nancy's wretched life, she knew with absolute certainty what had to be done.

She pulled her arm free, pivoted on her heels, and drove the stake deep into Iryna's heart.

The old woman gasped for breath and clutched her chest. "My dear sweet child, what have you done?"

As the sounds of the dying woman drifted up from the floor, Nancy lowered herself to the crib and took Nora in her arms. "Mommy's here," she said. "Mommy won't let anything hurt you."

Nora smiled up at her, a hint of red flashing behind her innocent eyes.

THANK YOU

If you enjoyed *He Comes in the Night*, please consider taking a moment to leave a review on Amazon, Goodreads, or your favorite website. Your thoughtful review helps other readers who might enjoy my work, and motivates me to continue dreaming up new stories.

For book updates, exclusive sneak peeks, and the opportunity to read advance copies, visit me online at: rickyfry.com

BOOKS BY RICKY FRY

He Comes in the Night
Lionshead
Bill and Ty Get High

www.ingramcontent.com/pod-product-compliance
Lightning Source LLC
Chambersburg PA
CBHW030326200626
46816CB00006BA/1948